HOSPITAL ACROSS THE BRIDGE

HOSPITAL ACROSS THE BRIDGE

BY

LISA COOPER

MILLS & BOON LIMITED
15–16 BROOK'S MEWS
LONDON W1A 1DR

First published 1982
Australian copyright 1982
Philippine copyright 1982
Large Print edition 1984

© Lisa Cooper 1982

ISBN 0 263 10571 7

Set in 18 on 19 pt Linotron Plantin
16–0684
Photoset by Rowland Phototypesetting Ltd
Bury St Edmunds, Suffolk
Made and printed in Great Britain by
Richard Clay (The Chaucer Press) Ltd
Bungay, Suffolk

CHAPTER ONE

'WHERE do you keep the other drums?' Sister Rosemary Clare asked, looking up at the sullen face of the nurse who was showing her the equipment in the operating theatre of the small private hospital.

'Those are the drums we always use, Sister.'

'But half of these don't even close properly. They aren't sterile.'

The older woman shrugged. 'They're all we've got. We've used them for long enough without anyone complaining,' she said, with a half smile that was intended to put the new and very young theatre sister firmly in her place.

'But what do the surgeons say? Surely they object to using unsafe equipment?'

'The surgeons? They like it as it is . . . Sister.' There was no mistaking the sneer in the slowly-added title and Sister Rosemary Clare flushed slightly.

What on earth made me take this job? she thought, and had an almost uncontrollable desire to tear off her immaculate cap and run for the stairs, to escape into sanity and the outside world.

'I'd like to see the instrument cupboard, Nurse,' she said, firmly. 'And after that will you please bring me the inventory list in my office?'

'I don't know where it is,' said Nurse Adams. She unlocked a glass-fronted cupboard and switched on the light that showed up the contents efficiently but with no dazzle so that the light would never interfere with the surgeon working at the operating table in the middle of the large and light room. 'Some of the instruments are in the steriliser. We had a case earlier and I haven't had time to dry them,' she added, anticipating the next question when she saw the new sister's eyes flickering over the contents of the shelves.

'I suppose we keep just a general set and a few extras, Nurse. I'm more used to having everything in the theatre ready for use. Do the surgeons bring their stuff in good time for preparation?' She tried to sound interested and friendly, but the wall of suspicion that had met her as soon as she was introduced to Nurse Adams showed no signs of crumbling.

'Sometimes . . . it depends. One or two rush in and expect everything done in five minutes.' Her large hands opened the next cupboard where row on row of surgical sutures and ligatures were stored with packets of swabs and rolls of cotton-wool and cases of plaster of Paris bandages. It was all neat and easy to see and was the first sight to make the new sister feel anything but apprehension and revulsion.

'You keep the cupboards beautifully,

Nurse,' she said and hoped her smile would be returned.

'I don't do them,' Nurse Adams said, shortly. 'Miss Nutford comes in here interfering and messes about in the cupboards.'

'Miss Nutford?'

'She's deputy matron and sometimes takes the odd case here.'

Sister Rosemary Clare raised her arched eyebrows and the candid green eyes were troubled. 'I don't quite get the picture, Nurse.' She glanced at her watch. 'Any chance of some coffee? I want to look through the desk in the office and get my bearings, and I'd like to have a chat about the theatre and the people who come here.'

'I've some coffee in the small steriliser,' said Nurse Adams, reluctantly.

'Then bring it in and have some with me,' Rosemary said. 'We have no cases today and I have a lot to learn.' There was a faint note of appeal in the low voice and a flicker of what might possibly have been warmth appeared in the pale blue eyes of the theatre nurse. 'But first, I would like the inventory list. If we can't find one we shall have to go through every piece of equipment and make a fresh one. I can't take over a theatre without signing a full inventory,' she said, firmly.

'The others didn't bother. They took it as it came,' said Nurse Adams.

'Why was that?'

'They weren't here long enough,' she said and flounced away to get the coffee.

Sister Rosemary Clare looked round her new domain with a sinking feeling in her heart. It was difficult to decide what was wrong about the place—there was such a lot that she liked and so many things that were glaringly bad. She thought back to her first impression. The entrance to the hospital was superb, being built in wide grounds set back from the quiet side road on the Somerset side of the Clifton Suspension Bridge. An air of affluence and care followed her as she entered the deeply carpeted hall and glanced up at the original prints and ornate mirrors of the main reception area. The solid teak desk gleamed dully, as if it knew that it had to prove nothing by shining with the superficial elegance of lesser pieces of furniture, and the fresh flowers in the Wedgwood vases were echoes of the gentle colours in the window curtains.

A heavy door concealed the waiting room which was more like a Regency salon than any waiting room that Rosemary had ever seen in a hospital, and the glossy magazines on the antique occasional tables were new and recent copies. Matron's office was set back a little, but had a window looking over the main sweep of the drive. That room again was beautifully furnished and more suitable for a hostess in a wealthy country mansion than for a hard-working Matron of a thriving private hospital, and the illusion was increased when the new theatre sister had arrived for her interview before taking up her new post.

'Miss Clare?' the older woman in the tailored navy silk dress advanced towards her, well-manicured hand outstretched.

'Yes,' said Rosemary and smiled, surprised and somewhat impressed by the muted opulence of the hospital.

'I'm very happy to welcome you to the Birchwood Hospital, my dear,' She settled Rosemary in a velvet-covered chair of soft chartreuse and rang a bell for coffee which appeared as if by magic, carried on a heavy silver tray by a girl in a dark dress and tiny maid's cap. 'Thank you, Doris,' said Matron and poured coffee into fragile cups, handing langues de chats and petit beurre biscuits.

Is this just for my benefit? thought Rosemary, a sparkle of amusement appearing in her usually serious gaze. If the rest of the hospital was as well-appointed, she would have the best job ever offered in a small hospital.

They talked about London . . . the theatre and the social life of Bristol and drank the fragrant coffee, and Miss Dundry, the matron, didn't mention the work for which Rosemary was being interviewed.

'Could I see the theatre, Matron?' The conversation was petering out and she was uneasy for the first time.

'I like to be called Miss Dundry, not Matron, and my deputy is called Miss Nutford. The other members of staff are called by their rank of course, but if and when one of the sisters is required to act in a more social way, first names are preferable.'

'I don't think that will arise, Miss Dundry. I know hardly a soul in Bristol and certainly no one here.' Matron gave her a sharp look. 'I would like to see the rest of the hospital, if it's convenient as I have to catch a train back to London,' she said.

'Very well.' Miss Dundry said it with

an air of tired uninterest. 'I'll show you a typical room and then we can go up to the theatre. You can't go in today as they are operating, but you can see it all through the observation windows in the theatre doors.' She led the way along the quiet corridor past more heavy doors and under elegant light fittings. 'The X-ray department,' she said, waving towards a closed door. 'Sister's office on the ground floor wing is there, and this is one of the rooms.' She flung open a door and showed a fresh, pretty room with a balcony and private bathroom, the bed table and foot stool and an empty drip stand being the only indications of it being anything but a luxury hotel room.

'How many wards are there, Mat . . . Miss Dundry?'

'No wards, only wings here, Miss Clare. We like to make our guests as comfortable as possible and keep them free from a hospital atmosphere as much as possible.' Miss Dundry sighed. 'I would like less surgery here, but we have many very good surgeons in the city and those who come from other counties who want to use our facilities, so we have to tolerate them.'

'But I thought that this was mainly surgical? In the advertisement it stated that this was a busy, short-stay surgically-acute private hospital.'

'Yes, it is, but we have some semi-permanent patients here also.' Miss Dundry frowned. 'Some of our . . . newer members of the board of governors would like to see us get rid of the long-stay people, but I would miss them very much and I shall fight to keep them. There are many matters on which I disagree with some committee members, but when decisions have to be made, I still make them in this place.' The sudden firmness with which she spoke made Rosemary aware that under the smooth elegance was a sharp mind and an egotistical desire for Miss Dundry, Matron of the Birchwood

Hospital, to get her own way regardless of the feelings and inclinations of anyone, but herself.

'The theatre?' asked Rosemary as Miss Dundry turned to go back along the corridor.

'Ah, yes, the theatre.' Miss Dundry tore her gaze from the embroidery on the pretty silk blouse that showed off Rosemary's soft curves, discreetly encased in the gathered bodice. Her eyes took in every detail of the slim hips, the long legs and the tiny feet of the new theatre sister. Her own hand smoothed the well-controlled contours of her own hips and tugged just a trifle impatiently at her too-tight belt. 'You're very young for such a position, Sister.'

They walked towards the lift at the end of the corridor. 'I was fortunate to have to do a lot of theatre work during my training, Miss Dundry. I gave you full details of my experience in the application and I have worked with many of Britain's lead-

ing surgeons.' Rosemary spoke with confidence, recalling her own expertise and
the high regard she knew existed for her
efficiency at the hospital where she had
received her training. 'I trained at the
Princess Beatrice Hospital, London, Miss
Dundry, and the standard there is very
high.'

The lift purred and stopped and along
the short white-tiled corridor, twin doors
and a side door confronted them.

'The side door leads to your office, the
double doors lead into a vestibule from
which the anaesthetic room and theatre
diverge. The surgeons' room is on the far
side of the theatre.' Miss Dundry looked
down at the floor. 'This was very expensive,' she said, with satisfaction. 'I think it
adds something, don't you? You'll like
the new chairs in the surgeons' room, too.
They are very comfortable.' She smiled.
'Not that I use them . . . I keep away from
the theatre as much as possible.' A door
swung open a fraction, as if someone was

about to emerge and then thought better of it. A waft of anaesthetic came from the theatre and Miss Dundry wrinkled her nose in distaste. 'You see what I mean?'

'It seems like home to me,' said Rosemary, laughing softly. 'I had begun to wonder if a theatre existed here at all. It's all so luxurious everywhere.' Her eyes sparkled. 'I can't wait to look round.' She walked to the round observation window and stared through at the scene inside. It was as she expected, a team of surgeons, a nurse gowned and masked and another figure in the small sterilising room at the side away from view, bright lights shining down on a prostrate form on the table and an anaesthetist sitting by the head of the unconscious patient. Her practised eye took in details of any equipment she could see beyond the draped trolleys. It was all there . . . all the essentials, but compared with the luxury of everything she had seen in the public part of the building, it was very basic and . . . dare she say it, old fashioned?

'Who is operating, today?' she asked.

'I think . . . yes, it's Mr Moody. He does hernias and cases that go home to be nursed after a day or two, and so he works very hard. He has two lists a week.' Miss Dundry sounded as if he was unreasonable to empty beds so quickly between operation day and admission day.

'And who is taking theatre before I or whoever you appoint takes over? I believe you said that the post came vacant because of sickness, Miss Dundry.'

'My deputy, Miss Nutford, takes theatre when you are off duty if there is an emergency.'

'And what about night duty? Who does theatre work at night?'

Miss Dundry turned away from the circles of light shining through the windows and walked briskly to the lift. 'Night duty?' she said, with a vague smile. 'We have few emergencies. Most of your work

will be planned cold surgery. Occasionally . . . very occasionally, you might
have to be there if there is a very ex-
ceptional case, but there is very little of
that here. I would, of course, make up
any time used and the off duty is generous.

Rosemary wanted to ask much more,
but there seemed to be nothing specific
that she should ask. It was clear that as far
as Miss Dundry was concerned the position was hers if she wanted it. The hospital was in lovely surroundings and
everything she had been shown was
beautiful, but she was swamped by the
plushness, and something intangible that
worried her.

'You have been very kind,' said Rosemary, 'but I mustn't take up any more of
your time.'

'When can you start?'

'I . . . when do you want me to come?'

'As soon as possible. As you know, our
other sister left in rather a hurry . . .

through illness, you know.' The brown eyes were suddenly hard.

She didn't like the last sister, thought Rosemary. I wonder why?

'I could be here on Sunday evening, ready for work on Monday,' she said.

'That's good. I shall leave the key to your flatlet in the house next door, with the receptionist, and you must ask her if there is anything you need. You will provide your own white dresses and shoes?' Rosemary nodded. 'Yes, I think we settled all that in our letters. Well, goodbye, and I hope that you will settle into our ways very quickly.'

The new theatre sister doodled on the pad in front of her on the old oak desk. The misgivings that she had experienced on the day of the interview were increasing with each minute she spent sitting waiting for the coffee that Nurse Adams was preparing. She started as the door opened and the nurse brought in a tray. 'Thank you. Now sit down and put me in the picture,' she said. Nurse Adams shifted her considerable bulk into a chair and handed a full cup of very good coffee to her. 'This is delicious,' said Rosemary and wondered why she was surprised.

'It's the surgeons' . . . nothing but the best for them,' said Adams with a slight sniff.

'That's what I find puzzling. Everything is so well-appointed but the theatre is badly equipped. Those drums for sterile dressings must have come out of the ark!'

'They're too expensive to replace,' said Nurse Adams.

'I would have thought they could have been re-shaped and plated for very little, compared with the cost of the tiles in the corridor outside, for instance,' said Rosemary.

The nurse didn't reply but sipped her coffee morosely. She watched the new sister open a drawer and take out a looseleaved book and examine it. 'That's the details of the visiting surgeons. Miss Nutford did it and we add anything fresh that they like,' the nurse volunteered at last.

Rosemary read the first name on page one. 'Mr Russell Nicaise, Orthopaedics.' There followed a list of instruments needed for simple procedures like pinning fractures and plating bone. She nodded. It was very much as she had seen in a similar book at Beatties, as the hospital in which she trained was affectionately called, and her mind warmed to the familiar. Next she read that Mr Nicaise had assisted at an operation in London where new techniques were being used in the replacement of hip joints and a list of instruments was stuck down in the book as if he had asked a record to be made in case he needed to refer to it in the future.

'This Mr Nicaise? Has he done this operation here? I take it that he's the local orthopaedic man?'

'One of them. Most of them do their

cases at the special unit in the Mendips, but he's fresh here.' Nurse Adams smiled maliciously. 'They all try it once here, and then we're back to hernias.'

'What do you mean? Has he operated here before?'

'He did one or two minor things like hallux and reduction of fractures but nothing big so far, except the one last week when he brought his own assistants.' She laughed. 'Miss Dundry was all over him. She told him that you were coming and could cope with anything he liked to bring in.'

'Did she?'

'She likes him for some reason . . . must have good connections or rich relatives. He seemed quite keen to do the one in the book.' She gave a derisive cluck. 'That should finish him here.'

'What do you mean? The theatre can cope with it. I've scrubbed for at least four of them and laid up the theatre for a good many more,' said Rosemary. Her disquiet grew. 'We'd better make that inventory, Nurse. Let's start in the anaesthetic room. You write down the items as I find them. I shall learn where everything is more quickly if we do it that way.' She thrust a notebook into the unwilling hands.

I shall have to start as I mean to go on, she thought. If I do my job properly, it must be all right here. But as she made the list and found several deficiencies in the normal theatre apparatus, her heart sank. In isolation, not one item was a dangerous exclusion, but added up, it made a less than perfect situation for working and a less than safe situation for staff and patients.

She made a second list while Nurse Adams was at lunch, listing the more vital things missing and making a pointed reference to the drums. She noticed that there were several new padded packets that could be used for containing sterilised swabs or instruments if the packet was autoclaved near to the time it would be used and discarded as unsterile as soon as the one operation was over. She put them on the bench in the sterilising room. Those at least would be suitable for use in an emergency or for anything requiring the utmost care and asepsis.

Nurse Adams came back from lunch and it was time for the new theatre sister to meet the rest of the sisters when they ate together. 'Will you take the instruments out of the steriliser and dry them so that I can check them against the inventory, Nurse,' she said. 'And could you tell me where the dining room is?'

'It's the second door in from Miss Dundry's sitting room. You know the door by the kitchen?' Rosemary nodded. 'Two doors along from there.'

Rosemary checked that her honey-blonde hair was neat under the small white cap and twitched the dark belt so that its silver buckle was dead centre and the clean white dress was trim. Nurse

Adams watched her leave, an expression of reluctant admiration mingled with pity giving her a more gentle look. She pursed her lips and opened the steriliser.

The dining room was austerely furnished with pre-cast plastic chairs and a long plastic-topped table. A sideboard that might have been smart in the era when flying ducks graced the walls of middle class families lay squat and forlorn against a white wall. Three sisters talked together in one corner and they stopped and stared when the new sister pushed open the door and stepped inside the room. Quietly, a good-looking girl a few years older than Rosemary came forward and held out her hand. 'I'm Sylvia Nutford, the deputy matron,' she said, and smiled. 'I can't say how glad I am to see you!'

'Rosemary Clare, and I think that Matron mentioned you yesterday when I arrived, and at my interview.'

'I'll bet she did,' said another woman in

a dark blue dress and rather fussy cap who was nearer to Miss Dundry in age than to either of the young women. 'Sylvia runs this place. Miss Dundry couldn't do without her.'

Rosemary turned to the other member of staff present, a humorous-faced woman in a tight white dress and no cap. She couldn't swear to it, but she thought the woman said, 'But we could do without Miss Dundry.'

'This is Rhona Brown, our visiting radiographer,' said Miss Nutford. 'Would you like to sit there. We all try to get to lunch together as this sitting is very much better than the earlier nurses' lunch. It is usually more convenient as most theatre lists are done in the early part of the day and all the consultants do their visits either before their hospital rounds or late at night when their other commitments allow. You'll soon get used to that part of the routine, while remembering that there isn't a set routine. We have to fit in when we are required, I'm afraid.'

'I believe that you take the theatre sometimes, if I'm off duty and the odd emergency crops up?'

Rosemary looked down to the radiographer, startled at her sudden burst of laughter.

'That's a good one. The *odd* case . . . has she been filling you up with the same old tale that all cases come in between nine and five?'

'Please . . . that isn't very kind, Rhona,' said Miss Nutford with a warning frown. 'In a way it's true. We do seem to get a lot of emergencies lately since two of the younger surgeons began coming here, but the work is very interesting and I'm sure you'll like both Mr Moody and Mr Nicaise.'

'Mr Moody was operating on the day I came for my interview, I believe. Were you scrubbed that day?'

'No, he brought a student from the hospital and I ran the theatre. I took theatre yesterday for Mr Nicaise. He inserted a Smith Peterson pin and it went well.' She passed the potatoes to Rosemary. 'I think it went too well.'

'Too well? How is that?'

'He was talking of bringing in a patient for a hip replacement, using a technique he saw in London, but quite frankly, I don't think I could tackle that, could you?'

'Why not? He'll bring his own instruments and we can do the rest. I take it the hospital is geared for portable X-ray for theatre use and there are monitoring sets . . . video for reference and enough staff for positioning the patient?'

Silence spread round the table. 'You aren't saying that you've seen one done?'

'If you mean the French approach that was perfected at the Princess Beatrice Hospital, London, I have scrubbed for four of them and laid up for several.'

'Well, don't tell him that,' said Rhona, getting up to fetch her pudding from the sideboard. 'He's fussy, and might think some of the equipment isn't all that it should be, especially for a case as important as that.'

'I've already made an inventory and noted any gaps. I think some of our things have been borrowed or lost as there do seem to be many items missing. I'll have to ask Miss Dundry for replacements and for some additional equipment.' Rosemary turned her attention to the food, suddenly embarrassed by the faint air of disbelief that greeted her words.

'How long do you think you'll stay here?' The other sister spoke. 'The last two theatre sisters stayed for two months each and couldn't get away fast enough.'

'This is Sister Ridge, in charge of the semi-permanent patients' ward on the first floor. She doesn't often have surgical cases so she has no real need to know . . . or to understand the difficulties of a new theatre sister,' Miss Nutford was apologetic and faintly critical of the other sister.

'I hope that you will like it here and I beg you to give the place a chance. In many ways, we have to battle against old-fashioned views and try to improve things, but the visiting surgeons and physicians are very good and usually appreciate effort when they see it.'

'When they see it,' muttered Sister Ridge, putting her chair back with a loud squeak and leaving the room, quickly.

'Well, I suppose I ought to be going back, too,' said Rosemary. 'Can I see you again today to ask about lists and surgeons?' Miss Nutford nodded. 'I'll go back and finish checking everything and then I'll know where everything lives. Could you come up some time before I go off tonight?'

'I'll come and have a cup of tea with you about four. You'll find cakes and biscuits in tins in your office, unless greedy Nurse Adams has scoffed the lot again.'

Rosemary walked slowly back to the theatre. It didn't make sense. The whole ambiance of the private hospital told of prosperity and well-being and yet in the places unseen by the patients and the visiting physicians there was penny-pinching and archaic apparatus. The theatre looked fine at first glance and to a busy surgeon who arrived when the trolleys were laid, the patient prepared for surgery and the one good case of instruments, lit discreetly and well in the background, making him take it for granted that everything matched in style and efficiency.

The sterilisers were old and caked inside with deposits from the hard water and the outsides could have done with a good scrub. The instruments laid out on a towel on the trolley by the cupboard were dull and filmed with the same water deposit, showing that they had been boiled for too long and kept in the steriliser instead of being cleaned and dried properly between lists. Rosemary pursed her lips. She had heard of theatres where this happened, the argument being that if an emergency came in there was a set of instruments sterile. But what if they just sat in the original sterile water and weren't transferred to a sterilising fluid? They could be cold and unsterile for hours.

'Who does the autoclaving?' she asked.

'We do,' said Nurse Adams, as she left for an afternoon off duty. 'It's down there.' She pointed to a door a few yards from the anaesthetic room. 'There's a batch of drums ready to come out,' she added carelessly. 'Might be a bit damp now . . . I forgot to take them out earlier. Do you want me to stay and do it?' She would resent being kept behind, the new sister could tell.

'No, I'd like to see it for myself. I've done some autoclaving as part of my theatre course and I ought to know how this one works before we need it urgently.'

Nurse Adams went down in the lift and Rosemary went to the autoclave room where a huge cylinder stood with a heavy door over its front. She inspected the pressure gauge and saw that it was down to nil, before unscrewing the bolts which secured the door while the steriliser was under a pressure of fifteen pounds to the square inch. As Nurse Adams said, the drums were damp on the outsides and as she put them on the rack, Rosemary wondered if they were safe to use. Had the drying process been done properly or at all? She went back to the theatre and took off her cap, replacing it with a theatre cap and mask and covering her dress with a clean theatre gown. At least there seemed to be plenty of clean linen in the cupboard. She went back and fetched the drums on one of the long trolleys used for carrying patients. 'I'll open a drum and see what it's like inside,' she said.

The drum lid lay back on bent hinges and she took a pair of single-ended instrument forceps with which to probe and examine the contents. She lifted out a packet of small swabs and put them aside, before closing the drum carefully, but noting that the lid didn't fit well. She turned and put the forceps back in their holder of disinfectant and picked up the swabs in her bare fingers. They were damp and quite unfit for use in a sterile situation. She looked for the tiny phial of coloured liquid that was usually to be found in sterile drums to test that the temperature had reached a safe level during the process of sterilisation, but found no such phial and so couldn't see whether the colour had changed to 'safe'. She tried to think whether the hospital had another type of reagent in a different packing, perhaps in a flat plastic container that she had missed when she searched through with the end of the sterile forceps.

A sound from the corridor made her step back from the drums. The outer doors swung furiously, the sense of urgency of the man striding into the theatre came as an unquiet breeze and the new sister was aware of a sudden apprehension. She saw a tall man with dark brown hair and deeply set dark eyes. He was handsome and compelling from his sleek head and firm, well-set shoulders to his taut-muscled legs and well-shod feet. The formal suit did nothing to hide the latent force in his bearing, the silk necktie seemed to imprison a restless spirit and the dark eyes blazed with controlled anger.

'Are you the only one on duty, Nurse?' he said. His face grew darker. 'I suppose they staff this place with casual labour . . . anyone free to be sent here whether they know anything about the work or not.'

'What can I do for you,' Rosemary asked, quietly.

'You? I doubt if you can do anything,' he said, curtly. 'I don't think you were here yesterday.'

'No, I wasn't here, but if you would tell

me what you want, perhaps I can get it for you.' He stared at her as if she was a fly on the wall . . . an unintelligent one. 'I *do* know where things are kept,' she said, mildly, but her eyes grew less hazel and more like the swirling depths of a green pool, as they did when her temper was rising.

'I want the sister who was here yesterday.'

'I think you mean Miss Nutford, the assistant Matron, who is coming here soon . . . in fact should be here at any moment.' She glanced at the clock and was half afraid that Sylvia Nutford would arrive and have to confront this bad-mannered and angry man. She thought back to the description given of some of the surgeons, and her lips, under the concealing mask, twitched. This must be Mr Nicaise . . . half French . . . that she could understand, but rather a pet? Oh, *no*, anyone keeping a pet as dangerous as this should beware of injury, of the deep hurt that those scornful eyes and blistering tongue could inflict.

'You must be Mr Nicaise,' she said.

'How did you know? I haven't seen you before.' His eyes lightened. 'She left it with you? Can I have it now, I'm in one hell of a hurry.'

'I'm afraid I don't know what you mean . . . there was no message left for you.'

'My retractor . . . the special one I use for hips. I can't do an arthroplasty without it.' He sounded petulant and thoroughly spoiled.

'Are you sure you left it here?'

'Of course I'm sure! Don't just stand there looking like a half wit! Look in the cupboards, and if you don't produce it in two minutes, I shall go downstairs and raise hell.' He scowled as she made no move to the cupboards. 'I've operated here once for an important case, but if, as I suspect, this theatre is badly run and has no permanent staff, I shall never book in a patient here again.'

'Your instrument is not here, Mr Nicaise. I have personally checked all the cupboards this morning and made a full inventory of every item in this theatre.' She thrust the neat copy of the inventory in front of him. 'You are welcome to look and see if any of those things are your property, but I would be grateful if when you come in here, you will at least be civil.'

'I don't know who you are . . . but you are much too young and green to be insolent to a consultant. I hope that you do not cross my path again.' He threw the list on the floor and swung away through the wildly flailing doors and down the stairs.

Sister Rosemary Clare picked up the list and put it on her desk. A bit of a pet, was he? 'Well, all I hope is that he keeps his word and never comes near the place again,' she said.

CHAPTER TWO

'COULDN'T you find the kettle? It's in the small cupboard. Nurse Adams should have shown you where to find it.' Miss Nutford stopped, and wondered why the new sister looked so miserable. Rosemary Clare stood by the wide window of the main theatre, staring out into the garden.

'I'm sorry . . . I was dreaming. The kettle has boiled but I turned it off until you came.'

'What's the matter?'

'Did you meet anyone as you came up?'

'No, but I didn't come up from the ground floor. I was with Mrs Chishome in the end room under the theatre, and I nipped up the back stairs.'

'You haven't seen Mr Nicaise?'

'No, has he been here?' She smiled.

'I'm glad you've met him. Nice, isn't he?'

'I thought he was damned rude,' said Rosemary, still smarting at the slighting way he had treated her. It was too bad. She *was* very young to have such a responsible post and she *did* look absurdly young in a trailing white gown, but who did he think he was, anyway? 'He was screaming for a retractor he swore he'd left here. He wouldn't believe that I hadn't hidden it . . . or thrown it out of the window, and he went off to rampage down to the office.'

Miss Nutford laughed. 'You mustn't take any notice of that. He does get worked up at times, I believe, but he's a very good surgeon and I suppose we have to make allowances for genius!'

'I've worked with the best there are and although they might get touchy when under stress, they weren't overbearing bullies to people they didn't know, and who could have no connection with anything that had annoyed them.'

'He was as bad as that?' Miss Nutford sat down and accepted a cup of tea and rooted in the biscuit tin. 'Nurse Adams must have hollow legs. There were at least a dozen chocolate ones yesterday after they had all gone, and now there isn't one.'

'He was bad tempered and as much as called me a liar.' Rosemary sipped her tea. 'Did he leave a retractor here? It isn't in the theatre or the surgeons' room. I made an inventory and I had another look after he left.'

'It went downstairs to the reception clerk and she might have forgotten to leave a note for him by the main entrance. He rushed off after his case and said he'd come back for his bag when the instruments were washed, and Nurse Adams said she found the retractor in the small steriliser. He dropped it during the op and it had to be boiled again in case it was needed again, but he was sewing up and didn't need it.'

'I'm glad he doesn't operate here very often,' said Rosemary. 'He's already labelled me a half wit—his words not mine—and I think I'd blow my top if he came here too often. He wouldn't be the cause of the last two theatre sisters leaving so quickly, would he?'

'No . . . not him,' said Miss Nutford, quickly. She shifted round to face the window and avoided the questioning glance of the new sister. 'It's rather awkward. I'm Miss Dundry's deputy and next in line if she leaves, but I find that I have conflicting loyalties.' She handed her cup back for a re-fill.

'In what way? Surely you both have the good of the hospital in common. Where I trained, that was drummed into us. We had to put the patients and the hospital before any personal feelings and tensions. It's hard at times, but it makes sense for everyone's well-being.'

'Miss Dundry . . . is a mixture. She has been here for ages, ever since this was little more than a private mansion where several rich physicians clubbed together to provide a very luxurious service for their plum patients. It was more of a social position in those days, with the matron inviting ambulant patients to her sitting room for bridge in the evenings with sherry and canapés as if she were entertaining private friends. Gradually, other doctors came . . . most of the old school retired or died and the new ones were more intent on healing than playing bridge!'

'And it rankles? I see, that explains a lot. She seems to have her priorities mixed. The chairs in the surgeons' room must have cost a bomb and yet we need several essential pieces of theatre equipment that might be needed at any time, urgently. I've made a list, by the way. Do I give it to you?' She put her cup down and fetched the packet of damp swabs. 'This worries me very much. I couldn't find the indicators to put in the drums before they're sterilised and this batch must be done again as Nurse Adams didn't slide the closures over the holes in the drums after they were sterile. I don't know how long they sat in that cold wet autoclave without having the closures made. The swabs were damp and I think she skimped the drying process before reducing pressure.'

'There should be a new lot of indicators. I sent down a chit last week. I had the same suspicions and I wanted to check.'

'I'm glad someone here feels as I do,' said Rosemary. 'But I couldn't find any.'

'They should be in a bright blue cardboard box, if they're anything like the coloured picture in the brochure.'

'In the brochure? Do you mean there weren't any here before you ordered them?'

'No . . . that's what I mean about divided loyalties. I had quite a row with Miss Dundry about the unnecessary expense and what was good enough for Sir

Tristram Maloney should be good enough for the other men. She said quite openly that they never used indicators and refused to send the drums for re-alignment.' The two young women stared at each other. 'But at least I got her to agree to sending for the indicators. Perhaps they haven't arrived yet.' She frowned. 'They should be here. We had an order from the wholesalers on Friday and they should have been included.'

'Was this the order?' Rosemary produced an invoice. 'I was going to leave this down in the secretary's office after I made sure that the stuff had arrived. Can you tell from the store cupboards what is new and what hasn't come? Whoever checked it in hasn't ticked the items off as having arrived.'

Miss Nutford gave a tired sigh. 'Nurse Adams again. Sometimes I wonder if she wants to drive away every efficient surgeon and every keen member of staff. Come to think of it, that's what she *has* been doing, whether it's intentional or not. We have many complaints from the surgeons, but Miss Dundry will hear nothing against her and ignores anything that she finds distasteful.'

'Like the smell of the theatre.' Rosemary laughed, recalling the expression of repugnance on the rather aristocratic face when she caught a whiff of ether. 'I suspect that Miss Dundry has not had a lot of experience of modern operating theatres?'

'She used to come up here for Sir Tristram's ENT lists sometimes. He still operates here once a week and you'll like him. He was a whole day here on Thursdays and does noses and any mastoids in the morning and tonsils in the afternoon. He brings his own assistant and instruments and leaves his case in the hall downstairs the evening before the ops so that everything can be prepared in time.'

'Sounds fine, but why does he bring his own assistant?'

'Most of the older men do as the theatre was never geared for staff to scrub for cases.'

'But Miss Dundry said I'd have two permanent staff and another when necessary. So far I've seen only Nurse Adams and I believe you relieve me when required?'

'There's a nursing auxiliary who had today off. Her name is Price, a nice little Welsh girl who is quite keen, but I'm afraid might be influenced by Nurse Adams who has so many short cuts in her work that it's a wonder anything gets done properly. If that girl isn't trained to do things thoroughly she will be a menace. She came two weeks ago and I find her willing and pleasant, but already she has the excuse that "Nurse Adams told me to do it this way, Sister" and I'm very glad you've arrived to take her in hand.'

'And I thought I was coming to run an efficient, acute surgical unit, not to have to train auxiliaries and have to fight for the right equipment. Are the indicators on the list?'

Miss Nutford frowned. 'They aren't here. There's no reference to them anywhere. They weren't ordered!'

'But that's terrible. Do you mean that whoever sent the order, deliberately left out something ordered by the deputy matron, after permission was given by the matron?'

'Put like that, it *is* serious. You'd better do those drums again . . . you know the drill? Twenty minutes at fifteen pounds pressure per square inch, turn to dry heat and take out after the pressure comes down.'

'I think it's the same method that I've used,' said Rosemary. 'What about gloves?'

'The dry glove steriliser is good. We had to have a new one as the old one was uncontrollable and even Sir Tristram complained, so it was replaced.'

'It sounds as if everyone takes it for

granted that they are going to be met by inefficiency and bad apparatus, but they accept it!'

'How right you are,' said Miss Nutford, as she left the theatre. 'I'll find out who cancelled this lot.'

The auto-clave came quickly to pressure. At least that part works, thought Rosemary. It was nearly time for her to go off duty for the evening and for Nurse Adams to come on and clean the syringe tray and check the sucker tubing. She heard the nurse coming back slowly, ten minutes late, just as she took the last drum out and closed the slots safely. Before she had sterilised this batch, she lined the drums carefully with a layer of gamgee tissue, the thick cottonwool making a protective lining that would keep the contents sterile for far longer than it might if the drums were faulty.

'Nurse Adams?' she called.

'Yes, Sister.'

Sister Clare checked her watch and

looked at the nurse. 'Have you the list for tomorrow?'

'No, Sister. You didn't ask me to get it.'

'I wondered . . . as you are late back, I felt sure that it had occurred to you to call in for it in the office. In future, whoever is off during the afternoon will fetch the list and any instruments from the office. Will you go and get them now, Nurse?'

'The morning . . . we don't need them yet . . .' The nurse let her eyes waver under the intense green of the thinly veiled impatience. 'Yes, Sister.'

'Go by lift as I want to get off duty. I shall wait until you come back as I want to see who is doing what and check with the book.'

Nurse Adams almost hurried for the first time, and came back with a heavy case of instruments and a list. 'Thank you, Nurse.' Rosemary scanned the list and smiled. Just two minor operations for removal of suspected rodent ulcers and two hernia operations. 'Have we the right pots for the specimens, Nurse? They will want to send the excised pieces for section.'

'If he wants that he'll have to bring his own.'

'No he won't! If anyone operates here, they should feel that we can cope with all their needs. I assume we *do* send specimens to the path. lab., Nurse?'

The mild sarcasm caused a dull flush to appear on the heavy face. 'Yes . . . there are some pots down in X-ray on the side.'

'Then please get them now and see that we have a regular supply sent up with the dispensary. By the way, where does the drug list go?'

'The hospital uses the local chemist for day to day needs and we send an order once a week to the wholesaler in the city.'

'Like this one?' Rosemary waved the invoice, and handed it to the nurse. 'Did you check this?'

'I put the things away.'

'That's not quite the same. Were they all there? You haven't ticked them off the list.'

'The gloves were there except for size eight.'

'But I assume that we have some size eights in stock?'

'No, Sister. We used the last in the last batch of sterilisation.'

'So if we use a lot, we can't replace them from stock?'

'It isn't my fault they didn't send them . . . all the other things were there.'

'We still need the gloves, Nurse.' Rosemary tried to speak gently. 'I see from the list that Mr Moody takes size eights and he is operating tomorrow. Have we enough sterile eights for him?'

'If not, he can wear a seven and a half. He has before now.'

'And he accepts that? Can you be comfortable in a half size too small?'

'He grumbles a bit, but Miss Dundry

doesn't encourage the use of too many different sizes. She says it isn't economical,' she added, defiantly.

'But if they need a certain size, they have to have a certain size, Nurse. By the way, I hope you have plenty of sixes? I take six and I cannot wear a six and a half.'

'No one ever wears six here, Sister. You must have very small hands.'

'I have, and I'm afraid that I shall want sixes, so will you sterilise a drum of packets containing size six gloves this evening, Nurse.' Nurse Adams opened her mouth to say something then thought better of it. 'We do have some in stock, I suppose?'

'We have half a dozen pairs left from some time back when a visiting surgeon came and telephoned that she would want some.' Nurse Adams almost smiled. 'She rang through and said that she knew we were the worst hospital in the West Country for that sort of thing, but would we see that she had the right gloves and the right kind of soluble sutures when she operated here!'

'And did you get the things she wanted?'

A half-smile answered her. 'Miss Dundry said to get the gloves, but she'd have to put up with the same kind of sutures the others used.'

'So what happened?'

'Nothing much. She thanked us for the gloves and then when she saw what she had for sutures, she threw one lot on the floor and swore. She finished her case and said she hoped she never had to work here again.'

'And you can smile at that?' The new sister was horrified. 'Doesn't it worry you that you sent her away thinking that this theatre is inefficient, just as Mr Nicaise does, I suspect.' She recalled the fury on the dark taut face, the deeply-set eyes that shone dark fire, and the set of the shoulders as he dismissed the theatre, the staff and the hospital as beneath his notice, to be left as quickly as possible and perhaps never entered again. She was amazed at her own reaction as his face floated before her subconscious mind. He hasn't given me a chance, she wanted to cry. How can he know anything about me, as a theatre sister, a nurse, or as a woman unless he comes back and gives me a chance to prove that I can run this department well, given the tools of my profession, the staff and the time to show what I can do? She thrust away the thought of anything more than professional success. She wanted to prove herself as a Sister. Did it matter what he thought of her as a woman? If he could look at her with respect, it would be enough, but she wondered idly how his mouth would be when he smiled, and if his eyes had golden glints of wicked humour when he was amused or pleased, or . . . in love.

'Are you going to scrub, tomorrow, Sister?'

'What did you say . . . ? Oh, yes, if Mr Moody comes alone. You will be here as runner, and the new nurse can be anaesthetic nurse. I'm going now. Miss Nutford is in the office downstairs if you need her, and I'll see you after breakfast tomorrow, here.' She smiled. 'I expect you'd like to lay up the first trolleys, Nurse. Tomorrow, I'll watch you and see what Mr Moody likes. Don't forget my gloves will you?'

She hurried away before something more could prevent her leaving. She wanted fresh air and time to think and the large suitcase in her room was still to be unpacked. There would be supper in the dining room, but did she want to meet the other sisters again today? She reached the front hall and smiled at the bland luxury that confronted her at every turn. Miss Dundry was talking to an elderly man with slightly stooping shoulders.

'Going off duty, Sister?' The smile was sweet and the man smiled too. 'Sir Tristram, this is our pretty new theatre sister, Miss Clare.'

'One of the Somerset Clares or do you come from Ireland, my dear?'

'Neither, Sir Tristram, I come from Essex, I trained at the Princess Beatrice in London and now I hope to get to know the West Country.' She smiled and he took her hand.

'Beatties, eh? Fine place . . . often went there when I was at Guys, and still know most of the ENT bods. Old Sir Horace still there . . . thought he died years ago but I saw his name on the list of a medical dinner last month . . . must be a hundred,' he said, cheerfully.

'Not quite a hundred,' she said, and laughed. 'It's just that he seems to have been there for so long, but he still operates on a few private cases.' It was good to speak to someone with at least a slight contact with her training school.

'Do you play bridge, Sister?' Rosemary sensed a change in Miss Dundry's attitude towards her, as soon as Sir Horace was mentioned. She's a terrible snob, thought Rosemary with a hidden smile. I'll have to drop a few names on occasion if I want to impress her. 'I have a bridge evening on Thursdays after Sir Tristram's list and we often need another player.'

'That's a lovely thought,' said Rosemary, 'but I'm afraid I didn't belong to the bridge club at Beatties and I've never learned how to play.'

I shall have enough of this place *on* duty without having to play cards in my time off! she thought. She decided that this might not be the best time to ask some of the many questions that had arisen from her work during the brief time she had spent in her new job. Tomorrow, I'll get things sifted and sorted out into what I can do and what is impossible to make function with the facilities we have here, she decided. I ought to try it as it is for a day or so and be sure of my facts before taking it up with Miss Dundry.

'By the way, Sister, any post for you comes here and not to the house next door. The house isn't always locked and mail left in the hall is vulnerable, so I advise you to tell your family to use this address . . . there are racks behind the secretary's desk for staff mail and telephone messages . . . but there is another public telephone in Birchwood Annexe where you have your room.'

'Thank you, Miss Dundry. I doubt if there's anything for me just yet. Half of my friends don't know where I am and I have a lot of letters to write when I have time.'

'I believe that we meet again on Thursday, Sister,' said Sir Tristram, with a warm smile.

'I'll look forward to that,' said Rosemary, and went into the secretary's office to find where she could expect any future in-coming mail to be. To her surprise, there was a pink memo slip torn from a pad, with her name on it. She read the telephone number she was asked to ring and gasped with surprised pleasure. Nick . . . Nick Tadworth, the surgical registrar in the orthopaedic unit at Beatties was in Bristol and wanted to see her. She grabbed the note and ran to the house next door, fumbling in her pocket for the loose change she carried in a tiny purse for emergency phone calls. The hall was empty and she dialled the number of the large hotel where Nick was staying.

Impatiently, she waited while the receptionist called his name on the tannoy and at last, his voice came over the line. 'Nick? It's Rosemary . . . What are you doing here?'

A pleasant voice answered her. 'Rosemary! How's my favourite nurse?'

'Sister, please . . . I've gone up in the world since I saw you last . . . or I thought I had,' she added.

'Not all as you expected? I *did* wonder when I heard where you'd gone.'

'You know the Birchwood? I thought you functioned in London.'

'I get around, hence this visit. I was asked to assist with a tricky hip job and to give a lecture to a batch of students on the new procedure with the joint replacement we've been doing. You know all about that one, and I can't tell you how much we missed you last week when we had one in orthopaedic ops.'

'Where are you now? Can you come here or is the hotel too far away? I'd love to see you.'

'No problem if you're off duty. I'll walk across and we can come back here for a meal and I'll walk you back again.'

'It can't be as near as that. I didn't see any hotels on this side of the bridge.'

'So, we walk across the bridge . . . fresh air will do us both good and it's a wonderful evening, or haven't you surfaced to notice?'

'Not really. I'll get changed and be at the end of the road in twenty minutes.'

She put down the receiver and let out her breath slowly. Dear Nick . . . just the person to see tonight when she was vaguely unsure of herself. She thought of what he'd said about missing her in the theatre. It was true. She was good at her job and when surgeons saw this, they forgot her slight, fragile appearance and learned that she was strong, efficient and quiet, good with patients and staff and made the operating theatre a place of cheerful achievement, free from unnecessary tensions. Only after hearing Nick speak did she realise how much her confidence had been bruised by the short time she had spent at the private hospital.

Rosemary opened the large case and shook the contents on to the bed in the huge room assigned to her. There had been no time to do much in the way of unpacking and she had seen the room only in artificial light and in the cold light of early morning. It was too big for a single bedroom and could have made a charming bed-sitting room, given the right furniture, but the narrow simple bed, the one wardrobe and chest of drawers of an unknown vintage sat in lonely isolation against plain white walls. The curtains didn't match the colours in the square of carpet that covered a token amount of wooden flooring and the light shade was cracked, giving a dark shadow line across the mirror of the unexceptional dressing table.

Quickly, she shook out a full skirt of white broderie anglaise and teamed it with a tobacco-brown silk shirt. The bronze sandals had rather high heels but gave her height and made the skirt swirl as she walked, showing the slender line of hips and waist. She brushed her hair vigorously and added a dash of bronzy pink lipstick to her soft mouth before catching up the bronze leather handbag that was a birthday present from a fashion-conscious aunt. She glanced out at the sky and draped a white angora sweater round her waist. She hurried down to the entrance and saw Nick coming along the tree-lined avenue. He grinned and waved and almost ran to meet her, catching her up and swinging her high like a child.

'Put me down, you idiot,' she said, laughing.

He dropped a tiny kiss on to the end of her nose and put her safely on the path. 'Am I glad to see you, Ros. I looked round that hotel lounge and thought I'd be bored out of my mind. I never thought you'd be free to come out.'

'Why not? Even downtrodden new sisters have to be let off the hook for air. Where is this place? I know nothing about Bristol and I'm longing to explore.'

'You came across the bridge when you arrived?'

She frowned. 'You mean the bridge down by the river that seems to join up all the main roads into Bristol?'

'No, the pretty one that you must have passed under. You know about the Brunel

Suspension Bridge, don't you?' As he spoke, they rounded the corner and through the heavy canopy of summer-green leaves, she saw a glimpse of tall towers and a dipping band of silvery metal from road to towers. They walked along the pedestrian way at the side of the road over the bridge and gazed down at the river. The full tide washed sluggishly against the stonework, and two boats waited for the swing bridge to open to let them through into the dock. A panorama of trees and distant fields was misty in the evening warmth and mingled gracefully with warm red brick and golden rock of factory and bond warehouse and the crags of the Avon Gorge.

'It's beautiful,' she said. 'I only wish I was sure I could stay here.'

'What do you mean? I had a peek and the hospital looks prosperous enough. Not afraid of it going bankrupt, are you?' He laughed. 'Must be great to have every-thing you want and no expense spared.

I've been to minor hospitals like this and nursing homes where the theatres were quite inadequate and anyone from Beatties would have a fit if they were asked to do anything more complicated than an appendectomy.'

'Watch carefully while I have a fit,' she said.

'Oh, no . . . you have to be joking. It isn't like that? It can't be.' They reached the other end of the bridge and were caught up in the summer crowds walking or sitting by the beautiful old bridge, then Nick led her down a sloping road to the hotel where he was staying. 'We'll eat and then talk shop, but first I want to tell you about Sue.'

All through the meal, he talked of Beatties and of Susan, his fiancée who was taking her final SRN exam in the spring. 'And we can be married as soon as she finishes midder. We have to wait until then if she is to have a job when we're married, and I shall miss her like hell, but we have to take the long view.' He grinned. 'And If I can take out her friends when I'm fed up and far from home, I shan't get into mischief,' he said.

'It's wonderful to see you, Nick. I was very depressed when I came off duty. Perhaps I'm imagining it, but I have a feeling that Miss Dundry wants to drive away all the surgeons except her old cronies who don't need the same rigid asepsis for minor things, or if they do, they rely heavily on antibiotics during after care. It wouldn't suit you as it is at present and I'm only too glad that I don't have a major op on my hands tomorrow. I want to get some things sorted out with Miss Dundry before I could be confident of anyone like you operating in that theatre.'

'Is it as bad as that? Surely the authorities wouldn't allow it to function if there was real cause for alarm?'

'It's fine for general surgery when the surgeon brings his own apparatus and special packs already sterile, and for most ENT, when it's impossible to work in completely sterile conditions as the inside of the nose and throat can't be rendered more than surgically clean. I'm looking forward to the list on Thursday with a dear old boy called Sir Tristram Maloney, but if someone wanted to do a major chest operation or a hip replacement, I'd advise them to bring everything including dressings in their own sterile packs. I may be too fussy, and I shall know better when I've done a test run on the drums when I have the right heat indicators in them.'

He raised his eyebrows. 'No way of knowing if the right heat is reached? That's bad.'

'And the drums shut unevenly. I've tried to bash two back into shape, but they need to go to a workshop or wherever they true them up after being dropped and dented.' She smiled and looked round the long, low bar where the carvery of the hotel displayed an inviting and delicious assortment of cold meats and salads, pasta and fried chicken. 'Let's forget the Birchwood and enjoy the evening, Nick. I think that an evening with you, and some food, will give me strength to do battle tomorrow.'

They chose lasagne dripping with hot garlicky sauce and Nick ordered a carafe of red wine. The bread was warm and crusty and they ate in near silence as they satisfied the first pangs of hunger.

'I had quite a good time out in the country today,' said Nick as he pushed back his empty plate. 'They do a lot of very impressive remedial surgery there and have a re-habilitation centre for children with congenital deformities. They even have ponies for them and find that they build up a terrific confidence in children who have never done anything adventurous because of their conditions.' He brought fresh fruit salad and cream to the table and ordered coffee. 'They have some new blood out there. I met someone I'd already seen in London when a group came to watch Henty do that last batch of hip jobs. I thought I'd seen this guy somewhere but I was scrubbed that day and had no time to look around much. He spotted me, to be precise, and asked me about Beatties.'

'What's he doing down here? Is he a London man?'

'No. He trained in Edinburgh and went to Canada for another degree. He's half French and very bright indeed. He says he's taken the junior consultancy in the Mendip place and is building up some private connections.'

'Half French?'

'Yes, he comes from Normandy originally . . . or his family did way back in the dark ages, and he has family connections with French Canada too.' Nick smiled. 'I think you'd like him, Ros. He's a bit like you. He works hard and doesn't suffer fools gladly.'

'Am I like that? I thought I was all sweetness.'

'You know what I mean . . . you're never belligerent, but your staff know that they have to do things right the first time.'

'I'm glad that this paragon and I differ in belligerence . . . or shall I say, bloody-mindedness?'

'Don't look at me like that Ros. When you flash that green glint at me, I know you are slowly simmering. Was it something I said?' He raised his hands in mock alarm.

'I think I met your friend and I didn't find him very pleasant. I saw him for just five minutes, but that was enough to convince me that he was a sarcastic bore. He may be an up-and-coming consultant, but I hope he doesn't have a case in my theatre for a very long time.'

'Steady, Ros . . . it isn't like you to condemn a person on such short acquaintance. What happened? Did he seduce you in the surgeons' room? No, you said five minutes . . . not really time was there?' He grinned as she blushed scarlet. 'Sorry, I was only teasing. Have some more coffee. It's very good and to make up for it, I'll buy you a Benedictine.' He waved aside her protests. 'You need a night cap and so do I. My brain is too active tonight after such a full day. You would have liked it, Ros. I'm here for two more days, in the Royal tomorrow and back in the country the next day. Any chance of you coming to watch? We could have a pub lunch or a meal back here in the evening. When is your day off?'

'I can't say, Nick. We have a full day list on Thursday and I haven't seen the lists for the rest of the week. I believe I have to fit in my off duty when there is a slack day as I have to be there to take everything that needs swab counts and the use of diathermy and any complicated apparatus. Better let it ride, but I'd like to see you again before you go back.' She found a notebook in her handbag and wrote out the telephone number of the hospital and added the number of the pay phone in the Birchwood Annexe. 'I can answer that if I'm there off duty, and if there is no answer, you'll know I'm not available. Better use that number unless there's a real emergency or a message that you can leave with the receptionist.'

She let the aroma of the liqueur tickle her nose. It was good to be with Nick and listen to his tales, relax with the man who was very much in love with her friend at Beatties. It was safe and pleasant, but as she looked round at the other couples, eating and talking, each pair engrossed in their own tiny world of a small table and each other, she was filled with a sadness that had in it nostalgia for times when she had thought she was on the fringes of love, and her pulse had quickened at the sight of a man with whom she thought she could spend her life. She was sad because she no longer missed Max, the man who wanted her to give up her career and be a housewife and mother with no connection with the profession to which she was committed.

Was the sadness only for him? She hadn't thought of Max for a year with any longing, she knew. Above the candle glow and the plush-covered chairs, she saw a dark face with deep-set eyes that seemed to burn through the smoke-misted air of the bar, hovering like the face of a genie in a fairy tale. A lurch of recognition made her heart contract, sending bright colour to her face.

'Well, it seems that you might have to meet your *bête noir*, again . . . and sooner than you expected, Ros; he's coming over to speak to me.'

CHAPTER THREE

SISTER Rosemary Clare put a hand to her throbbing head and leaned her cheek against the cool window of her office. Behind her, she could hear the swish of the long-handled mop as the new assistant nurse washed the floor of the theatre. The extractor fan in the sterilising room was not working properly and she had dried the freshly cleaned and boiled instruments in a hot and steamy atmosphere, finally bringing the instruments into her office to finish them and pack them into the heavy case that Sir Tristram had brought to the Birchwood Hospital the night before his list.

She pushed back a strand of hair that had escaped from her theatre cap and walked into the sterilising room again.

She flung open the window and watched the steam spiral away into the evening air.

'Ah, I see you managed to open the window, Sister,' said Sir Tristram, coming in to say goodbye. 'Was it stuck? We usually have it open during the list unless the weather is very cold.'

'But surely, with sterile trolleys and instruments exposed to the air, we can't do that? I thought that the air-conditioning was broken. Is it always like this, Sir Tristram?'

'Ever since I can recall . . . no, that's not true. It went wrong about two years ago and Miss Dundry said it couldn't be repaired.' He looked thoughtful. 'I suppose it should have been done, but it never bothers me unless the theatre fills up with steam when we are blacked-out for some cases.'

'I couldn't possibly leave the window open with the theatre working, sir. Look across there.' He leaned against the window sill and sniffed the air. 'Over there.' Rosemary pointed to a pillar of smoke.

'Someone must be burning old tyres by the smell,' he said, with mild interest, and the new sister realised that however charming he might be, Sir Tristram was going to be of no help at all in her fight against conditions in the operating theatre of the Birchwood Private Hospital.

'You look tired, Sister. I hope I haven't been too demanding?' He beamed at her. 'I did enjoy my first list with you. I like a quiet theatre and you certainly know how to run an ENT theatre. I shall tell Miss Dundry how well we got on together.' He picked up his bag. 'Pity you don't play bridge, my dear.'

'I'm not tired, just hot. I'm going off duty soon and I can get some fresh air,' she said, smiling. Just because he couldn't see anything wrong with his nice comfortable hospital, it wasn't enough to make her cross with him, personally.

She tidied her desk and went to inspect the rest of the department. Nurse Price had done well and she had taken Nurse Adams's place during the afternoon list while a nurse from the ground-floor wing was coping with the anaesthetist and Nurse Adams was off duty. It had been a good day as far as human relations went, but the nagging thought that the theatre was not equipped as it should be for the safety of the patients was ever present in the mind of the new sister.

I'm tired and hungry, she thought and wondered if Nick Tadworth was back from the orthopaedic hospital in the Mendips. Her pulse quickened. He would be with Mr Nicaise, the young surgeon who she remembered with such distaste. What did it matter? At least he had no idea that the girl who was with Nick Tadworth in the carvery of the hotel was the same girl he had been rude to in this theatre the day before she met Nick. She half-smiled, recalling her near panic as the dark-eyed man advanced towards them, two nights ago as they finished their meal and sat sipping coffee and liqueurs.

'Don't mention who I am, Nick,' she hissed as Mr Nicaise came nearer.

'If you say so,' said Nick, amiably. 'Hello Russell. What brings you to the Cliffside?'

'It's a free country and I was hungry.' The dark eyes smiled and looked at Rosemary with warm appraisal.

Nick shrugged as if to say he had to make some kind of introduction. 'This is Rosemary,' he said, simply.

'Haven't I met you somewhere?' said Russell Nicaise.

'I can't think where,' she said, airily. 'Are you a friend of Nick's?'

'Same trade. But that wouldn't interest you. You haven't finished here, I hope. Let me get you another of those.'

'No more,' she said. 'I ought to be getting back, Nick.'

'Have a soft drink . . . I would be

grateful if you'd stay for another ten minutes. I want to talk to Nick about something, if you don't object . . . that is if you can spare him. I promise not to talk shop for more than ten minutes. I know how boring we can be if the lady is not involved in our line.' He smiled, showing perfect teeth in a wide, generous mouth. 'And you are much too pretty and petite to be a woman doctor.'

'I'll have a beer, if you're getting them,' said Nick. 'You can spare a few minutes, can't you, Ros? I'll take you home in good time to get your beauty sleep.'

'Very well, may I have some orange juice?' she said. She watched the broad shoulders as Mr Russell Nicaise made his way to the bar. 'Amazing,' she said, flatly. 'Quite civilised, isn't he?'

'Come on, Ros . . . he's a really nice guy. Tell him who you are. It might help when he comes to your theatre again.'

'I don't think it's necessary. It would embarrass me and would be of no interest to him as he isn't coming to operate at the Birchwood.'

'At least let me tell him you are a friend of Sue's. He thinks you're my girlfriend and he might like to date you himself if he knows you are just a friend.'

'I need that like I need a hole in the head,' she whispered, as Russell Nicaise came back with a loaded tray.

'Hope you don't mind,' he said, with a charming smile. 'I've had very little food today and I can eat while we talk.' He gave Rosemary a tall glass filled with fresh orange juice and ice and smiled. She lowered her eyes before the intent and very interested glance. 'I'm sure I know you,' he said '. . . those lovely eyes with those fascinating emerald depths.'

She blushed slightly and tried to tell herself that it was because she was annoyed. He was pushing his luck by being so obvious. His good looks must give him the idea that every girl he met and purred over must succumb to his considerable charm. If she could convince herself that he said such things to every woman he met, she was half way to regaining her first impression of him. The slightly arrogant lift to his jaw as he beckoned a waiter to bring more rolls and butter reassured her that he was the same self-opinionated man who had stormed into her presence such a short while ago, but the smile he projected towards her when he asked if he could order more orange juice was hard to equate with the monster that she met and disliked.

'I saw a case today that is a classic, Nick. He's had one hip replacement done in the States but wasn't happy with it. One of the creaky ones. His other side needs doing badly and he wants it done in the West Country as his wife and family are here.'

'Where was this? In the Royal in out-patients?'

'No, I saw him privately. I was asked to add my opinion and consulted with his private doctor and Sir Alec Perivale who is here for a conference.'

'Old Perry here . . . what will Harley Street do without him?' Nick laughed and looked at Rosemary, but she shook her head in warning. She knew Sir Alec well and had worked with him on several occasions, but she had no intention of telling Mr Nicaise who she was.

'Yes, he was very interested. He said it was similar to one case he had done at the Princess Beatrice Hospital a little while ago. He asked me to assist if we can find a bed in a private nursing home that can cope with that kind of work.'

Rosemary felt stifled. She wanted to walk out and not hear what was said, but she was rooted to her chair. There were other surgical nursing homes in the area . . . they could go to one in Bristol itself or one on the Downs . . . Bath wasn't far away and some of the hospitals had private rooms. They would find a room and a theatre that would suit them, without having to come to her, however much she wanted to assist Sir Alec again.

'Have you a bed, or isn't it as urgent as all that?' said Nick. 'I'd like to look in if I can manage it.'

'It's difficult. The main hospitals are short of staff due to an epidemic of food poisoning and two of the best anaesthetists are on holiday. They say that Bruce Hatton is very good, but he insists on having the last week in July off and the two weeks at the beginning of August to take his large family away on holiday.' He frowned, impatient of snags and, Rosemary thought, resenting anyone having a private life that interfered with his august wishes.

'He's back in Bristol. Saw him today. His youngest had mumps when they were camping in Scotland and he thinks the others will go down with it, so they came home. He says he'll take some more leave in a week or so when he knows if the others are going to be all right. He's very good.'

'That's fine. Now, all we want is a bed. I tried the convent but they are full. The other major nursing home has some surgical wards closed for painting.' He shrugged. 'It only leaves one place as far as I know, unless you have other ideas, Nick.' He drained his glass. 'It will have to be that dump, the Birchwood . . . the hospital over the bridge.'

Nick shuffled his feet uneasily, as he saw Rosemary bend to pick up a paper table napkin from the floor, hiding her shock and anger. How dare he condemn the place on the strength of one implied mistake . . . which was his fault as much as anyone!

'I'll give it some thought, Russ and ring you. You're staying at the medical school, I believe.' Nick smiled at Rosemary. 'I must take Rosemary home, now.'

'Thanks, Nick,' she said. 'I'd like to go, now.'

Mr Nicaise stood while she gathered up her jacket and bag, his eyes taking in the details of her slight but rounded figure and the slender curve of her tiny feet in the absurd sandals. 'Have you a car?' he said.

'It isn't far to walk,' she said, quickly. 'I like walking.'

'It must be just round the corner if you intend walking in those very pretty and quite useless shoes,' said Mr Nicaise. 'I could drive you.'

'It's only across the bridge,' she said, and stopped, afraid of saying more. He gave her a long, cool look and she could almost see the question racing in his brain as he registered again that he had seen her somewhere. 'Thank you for the drink,' she said and walked away, ignoring his hand which he raised to take hers in farewell.

'Wait for me,' said Nick in an aggrieved voice as he caught her up outside the hotel. 'He isn't coming after you.' He took her arm. 'Calm down, ducky, he isn't as bad as that and when he comes to your place, you'll both laugh about this.'

'It will be hell!' she said, firmly. 'He will be quite insufferable, and the worst of it is that he will have cause to be angry if we can't cope or we fall down on our asepsis.'

'I'll try to find out tomorrow before they book the case in, Ros, and meanwhile press on with that stupid woman in charge and try to make her see sense. I have to go back to London this weekend, but if I have the chance to come for that case, I can scrub for him and help you out in any way you like. I want to see this one, anyway,' he added as she squeezed his arm, gratefully.

'Bless you, Nick. I'll concentrate on the lists we have booked. At least I know that he can't come before next week as we have a general list tomorrow and ENT on Thursday.'

'You still have Friday, or even Saturday. A lot of private work is done on Saturdays.'

'I have to have a day off sometime. I hoped it would be Friday, and the nurses clean up at the weekend in any civilised theatre.'

'What about emergencies? You can't be there all the time.'

'Miss Nutford, the deputy matron, takes them if I'm off. It could work quite well once I get organised and the surgeons no longer take it for granted that Birch-wood is some kind of dirty, badly run abattoir.'

'He really gets up your nose, doesn't he? Can't think why. You've had your share of tetchy surgeons throwing swabs around, haven't you? What makes him any different, or are you getting ultra-sensitive now you are in sister's uniform?'

'I think I'm worried, Nick. I hate in-efficiency and this could be dangerous. I'll be happier when I know what's happen-ing in those drums.'

And the drums had been the cause of her headache on this, the third day of her work at the Birchwood Hospital. First of all, Miss Nutford had told her that it had been Miss Dundry who had cancelled the order for the chemicals to show if the autoclaving was complete and the drums efficient. The new sister had asked Miss Dundry if she could have the phials re-ordered and was given very reluctant permission to tell the secretary to telephone an urgent order for them, when the older woman saw that there was a glint in the young sister's eyes that would mean trouble if she didn't concede something, but she firmly refused to have the drums sent away, one at a time, for treatment, saying that the odd-job man was quite capable of straightening a few drums.

The gloves were mentioned and Rosemary had the impression that she had no right to have small hands and take size six gloves when most of the women scrubbed in the theatre took sevens, and when Miss Dundry swept away to the consoling elegance of her own private sitting room,

Rosemary knew that even if she had gained a slight victory there were many battles to be fought, and the woman who had ruled the hospital for so many years would fight every inch of the way to preserve the old habits and peaceful ways of the hospital.

The odd-job man had arrived while Rosemary was at lunch on the day of Sir Tristram's list, when the trolleys for the first two cases of the afternoon were ready and the theatre was spotless. He walked in, wearing dirty overalls, with mud-caked shoes from a session in the garden, and marched into the sterilising room, brushing against one of the trolleys and wearing no mask. The new theatre sister came back just in time to see him pick up one of the swab drums and open the lid, trying to true up the lid with the base.

Through gritted teeth, Rosemary told him to take the empty drum down to his workshop and to leave the theatre quickly before he made anything unsterile. She

was conscious of the smirk on Nurse
Adams's face as she saw her new senior
nearly lose her cool, but she managed to
be polite to the man and to gain his co-
operation with his promise to tackle one
drum a day as they came empty.

And so the day had ended, with tiny
pinpricks of discord between Nurse
Adams and Nurse Price, who no longer
looked on Adams as her private oracle
and asked Sister Clare for instructions.
Slowly, painfully, a glimmer of success
came through the blank wall of indiffer-
ence and as Sir Tristram had said, everything went well as far as the theatre atmosphere was concerned.

As she went off duty, Rosemary looked
to see if there were any messages, but her
slot was empty. She went to change from
uniform and while she was in the bath, she
heard the telephone ring. It rang and rang
in the empty house as none of the other six
members of staff who lived there were at
home, and Rosemary swathed her body in

a large towel and hurried down to answer it. It can't be for me, she thought, as Nick would have left a message earlier if he was going to be free for the evening. The towel nearly slid from her hand as she heard the voice of Miss Dundry.

'Ah . . . I thought I might have missed you, Sister. I'm afraid there's an emergency. Can you come back on duty and see me in my sitting room in half an hour?'

'But I thought that Miss Nutford took emergencies when I am off duty, Miss Dundry. I have been on duty all day and I was in the bath when you rang.'

'I'm sorry, Sister, but there is no alternative. Miss Nutford is out and Mr Moody says that this case can't wait until the morning.'

'I'll be there, Miss Dundry,' said Rosemary, and raced back to her room. The instinctive response to any emergency made her forget that she should be off duty after a full day in the theatre and she dressed quickly in uniform, brushing her still damp hair back under the cap she had thought could be discarded and sent to the laundry. The bath had freshened her, but she was hungry. I'll lay up for the case and pop down for staff supper if there's time, she thought.

Nurse Price was walking along the corridor in front of her when she reached the top floor. 'Miss Dundry caught me, Sister. She said I had been off duty this morning and that I was on call. I thought I'd better check with you before leaving the building.'

'You live out, don't you, Nurse?'

'Yes, Sister. I come here on my moped, so it's all right if I have to stay late. May I ring my parents and say I shall be late?'

'Come up to the theatre first and I might be able to give you some idea of the time you can go. I'm sorry about this, Nurse.' Rosemary smiled. 'But I'm glad to have you to help me. I thought you did very well today with Sir Tristram.'

The girl looked pleased. 'I enjoyed it.

My first impressions here rather put me off doing my training, but I think I might apply for a place in a training school after all.'

'Good for you. In spite of this kind of annoyance, it's a good life and very satisfying.' Rosemary heard herself saying all the things she had believed in until she came to the Birchwood, and she knew in her heart that for her they were still true or she wouldn't care what happened in the hospital, or how badly run the surgical side could be.

From the theatre, she rang down to Miss Dundry's sitting room and told her that she had put the general set of instruments in to boil and asked if she had any news of the patient. Miss Dundry was vague about the man's condition but said that Mr Moody would be coming in to see the man again and to operate in an hour. 'I think he said it's an appendix, Sister, but he'll tell you more when you come.'

'Nurse Price and I are going down to

supper. We have eaten nothing since lunch and we need some food,' Rosemary said, firmly. 'The instruments are in to boil and we can lay up when we know if there are to be any extras. If Mr Moody comes in, will you ask him to contact me either in the dining room or here?' Her voice was crisp and Miss Dundry agreed weakly, as if it was all too boring for her to deal with.

'Come along, we'll feel stronger if we eat,' said Rosemary. 'I can slip back and lay up the trolley if you will go straight to the anaesthetic room and test the cylinders.'

They ate shepherd's pie and cabbage and Nurse Price contrasted the food with the menu presented to the patients at each meal: more economies for the staff while the visiting doctors and patients thought the whole place was luxurious! Rosemary pushed aside her apple pie and custard and said she'd lay up the theatre.

She worked swiftly and quietly with the

easy assurance of one who knows exactly what she is doing. The sucker tubes from the afternoon tonsil list were hanging from a hook to drain and she took two to put in the smaller steriliser in case the appendix needed clearing of exudate as it certainly would if there was acute inflammation or perforation. She ran the tubing through her fingers to make sure that there was no free fluid inside and her sensitive touch came to a soft obstruction. She took the tubing to the tap and forced water down to flush the whole length of the tube. Her face darkened. It was blocked with tonsil goo, and if it had been boiled the soft mess would have hardened and made it impossible to use successfully.

'Who cleaned the tonsil sucker, Nurse?'

'I cleaned the collecting bottles and Nurse Adams said she'd do the tubes.'

Silently, Sister Clare showed her the sudden gush of dark red blood and discharge that came from the end of the tube. Clear water followed it and Rosemary put the tube in to boil.

'Oh!' said Nurse Price.

'I'm glad you saw this, Nurse. It proves that we have to be thorough in all things and leave nothing to chance. If we have a burst appendix, as I suspect is the case tonight, the surgeon will want a sucker used in a hurry to prevent the free discharge from contaminating the peritoneum and causing complications. If he was handed this, the discharge would flow unchecked and be impossible to clear with swabs, or packs.' She picked the long metal sucker ends from the steriliser where the other instruments were boiling and put them under the cold tap. A wire, kept for cleaning the inside of the metal, went through easily. 'Who cleaned these, Nurse?'

'I did.' The blue eyes were wide over the mask.

'And you did them properly.' Rose-

mary slipped them into the second steriliser with the rubber tubes. 'They will do
later. I'll lay up this trolley first and check
your work and then we can only wait.
Let's put some coffee on to percolate.
We'll all need some before the evening is
finished. Go and ring your family. If we're
very late, you should sleep here. I know
there's a spare room in the Annexe and it
might be better if you stay and don't have
a journey to make when you're tired.'

'Thank you, Sister. I'd like to do that.'
She went down to the hall to telephone and
came back with a slip of paper. 'Mr Moody
is here and sent this for you, Sister.'

Rosemary glanced at it and was glad
that she had taken theatre for him for his
hernia list on Wednesday. 'Dr Hatton is
the anaesthetist,' she said. 'Have you met
him, Nurse? We had Dr Fortune for the
two lists I've seen.'

'He's very good, Sister. All the
surgeons prefer him. The patients like
him, too.'

'And the staff?'

'I like him, but he treats us all as if we are a part of his family. I believe he has six children and he can't forget them when he comes here.' She laughed. 'I sometimes think he will tell me to go and clean my teeth or make sure I washed behind my ears, but he's very nice.'

'That's a relief. I couldn't stand an overbearing type just now. I know Mr Moody and I liked him a lot, so we should be fine.' She read the rest of the note. 'He thinks it might be an appendix on the point of bursting, so he's ordered the premedication drugs and hopes to begin at ten-thirty. We have time for coffee and biscuits. I now know why the biscuits disappear so rapidly. That pudding wasn't exactly appetising, was it?'

They sat in the surgeons' room in the comfortable new chairs and relaxed. Nurse Price was surprised that she was allowed to do so, but as Rosemary pointed out, they were there for an emergency, having done their duty and more, and they needed to be fresh and composed when the rush started. The porter brought intravenous fluid and said that blood would be arriving from the blood bank if needed. At least they jump to it when the surgeons order something, she thought. 'I'll telephone them direct if we need it,' she said, 'but it's more likely that we'll need saline or plasma.'

'That's what Mr Moody said,' said the night porter. 'Anything more you want, Sister?'

She warmed to the homely-looking man who evidently approved of a little more efficiency than his daytime counter-part. 'No thank you, but may I phone if I get stuck?' She smiled, sweetly.

'Anything at all, Sister. I heard you were stirring things a bit . . . and I hope you do. This place needs someone like you. You must stay, even if it's a bit up-hill at first.'

'Thanks, I hope I can. Just one thing.

Have you had any wound infection here in the last two years?'

'What have you heard, Sister?' He sounded more cautious. 'I can't really say.'

'I'm a bit worried about the drums,' she said. 'I'm having them repaired gradually and only using them for one list before re-sterilising and they seem all right if I do that. Now that I have the test phials I feel more secure and I'm supervising all sterilising at present, but I can't help feeling that, at some time, the necessary procedures were not kept going and there might have been trouble.'

'I shouldn't say this, Sister, because it was all hushed up, but two surgeons nearly sued the place last year and haven't been back with any patients. They couldn't prove anything and Miss Dundry said it was cross-infection in the convalescent home they were sent to after three days here, but there was trouble.' He sighed. 'I like a bit of action. I was in the navy and saw it there and I thought this was mainly surgical when I came three months ago.' He grinned. 'I like the place but get a bit fed up with the regulars. More like a blasted hotel than an acute surgical unit, if you ask me. All I've said is hearsay . . . don't quote me, but you've been here about five minutes and you've heard something, too,' he added, shrewdly.

'Thank you, Mr Bryant,' she said.

'That's another thing . . . you take the trouble to address everyone by name . . . they don't all do that. Mr Nicaise does . . . but we shan't see him again either.' He swung open the door and pushed the theatre trolley to the lift.

Mr Nicaise? Why single out the one man who in her opinion was the one who *did* lack manners when addressing staff. Perhaps he's better dealing with porters . . . men who don't like being bullied, she thought.

Nurse Price stood rather nervously by

the anaesthetic trolley and listened for the whine of the lift. Mr Moody was bringing a student to scrub for him and he arrived five minutes before his boss. Sister Rosemary Clare introduced herself and watched his relief as he found that there was a new, crisp-looking sister in charge and that she had some gloves that fitted him. 'I came once and had to cram my hands in a size too small,' he said. 'They split and I used three pairs to the annoyance of the sister before you, who said they were short of gloves. They were short of everything, but this is more like the teaching hospital set-up.'

'It ought to be. I'm fresh from a London hospital,' she said. 'Bear with me . . . you're right about equipment but I think we're winning.' It did no harm to spread a little of her own propaganda, to go back to the Bristol teaching hospitals. 'I hope that we can encourage some of the men who disapprove of the place to give it another chance.'

He was scrubbed and ready when Mr Moody arrived and the patient was on the table. The surgeon looked round and sensed the indefinable quality that makes a good theatre, and smiled. 'All ready, Sister? Sorry that you had to come back on duty, but Miss Dundry says that you don't mind how many emergencies you have as you need the experience.'

'You must be mistaken, Mr Moody. I had a lot of accident work at Beatties and worked in each of the theatres! I came here fully prepared for anything in surgery and find that I am expected to fit in almost as a relief staff!'

He seemed surprised and she made a silent vow to make sure that everyone who came to her department would be aware that she was *not* just a very young woman with no experience worth mentioning.

'That's interesting. I bring minor things here as a rule. The patients like it here and I would like to bring more, but the surgical side has never impressed me very favourably.'

She took a deep breath. 'Conditions never improve until you insist on what you want, Mr Moody. If you went to Miss Dundry and spelled out the equipment and improvements that are essential, she would have to listen. I have been doing my best in the three days I've been here, but there are aspects that worry me, too, and I can do little without the backing of the medical staff.'

He stared at her. 'You are quite right,' he said, slowly. 'We all let it slide and then opt out rather than complain.' He grinned. 'We don't all join the bridge parties, but I suppose we are cowards and hate to upset the friendly social atmosphere downstairs. But I promise I'll do my best when we have the next meeting of governors.'

As soon as the first incision was made and the sucker was connected to the pump, Rosemary had time to look at the anaesthetist. He was a man of about forty, with thinning hair and kind eyes and his touch was gentle as he passed the intra-trachial tube through which the anaesthetic gases would flow. The patient was relaxed even though the anaesthetic was light. The form of curare used to relax the internal muscles made the work of the surgeon easy and there was no spasm to interfere with the exploration. The appendix was exposed and the surrounding area packed with warm saline towels to catch any discharge, and the sucker hissed like a waiting snake. The row of used swabs sat neatly on a rack and the numbers of checked swabs were clearly marked on a blackboard at the end of the theatre.

Rosemary glanced round the theatre and was pleased with what she saw. The preparations had been adequate, the surgeon was happy and the anaesthetist sat by the head of his patient with the drip canula firmly stitched into a vein in the arm of the patient.

Mr Moody took an atraumatic needle with the catgut incorporated so that as the needle was pulled through the delicate membrane, it wouldn't tear it, but flow through the tiniest hole possible and make a sealed join. He encircled the inflamed base of the swollen appendix, making a purse string, and gently pulled it half closed before cutting between the two firmly placed Spencer-Wells forceps that held the appendix. He dropped the appendix and one pair of forceps into the waiting kidney dish and hesitated. 'This man is allergic to penicillin, Sister. I can't give him an umbrella course, so we'll have to keep praying!'

'Are you going to cauterise the stump, Mr Moody?'

'Have you any pure phenol?' She held out the tiny jar that she already held in her hand, so he could see the label. 'Good . . .' He smiled and dipped a sterile probe into the pure acid and carefully touched the raw stump before pushing it gently down through the purse string and pulling the suture tight and stitching it down. The inflamed stump was no longer in contact with the lining of the peritoneal cavity and the risk of infection much less, as any organisms from the infected stump would go into the gut and be excreted. Sister Clare stood ready with a powder insufflator.

'What? More good ideas?' he said.

'Some of our surgeons still use sulphonamide powder in cases like this and more are returning to it in preference to some of the antibiotics. I ordered some in case it was called for.'

'That's fine . . . can you puff it in there . . . and there. It might help prevent adhesions forming, too. Thank you, Sister.'

Dr Bruce Hatton took out the trachial tube as the last skin suture went in and the patient stirred. 'Do you know anything about Mr Russell Nicaise?' he asked.

'I've been here for only three days,' said Rosemary.

'Have you heard of him, Clive? He wants me to help when he does a new hip replacement job here. Is he any good?'

'He has had a lot of contact with some of our leading men, but I haven't seen him in action. Is he doing the whole thing?'

'No, he has Sir Alec Perivale coming, but he says he will be doing most of it as he has already assisted many times and wants to be sure he can do it alone if he goes to Canada.'

'Not stopping here?' Bruce Hatton grinned. 'Must be footloose and fancy free. Can't imagine ever leaving Bristol, let alone Britain with my family, and when they fly the nest it will be too late.'

Rosemary listened and said nothing. Her stomach had turned over at the thought of Mr Nicaise glaring at her once more in her own department . . . but her heart had a dull ache at the thought of him leaving Britain for Canada. She recalled what Nick had said, that Russell Nicaise had connections with French Canada.

'He's half French, I believe,' said Clive Moody. 'Probably trained here and wants to get back to all those dark-eyed beauties in Quebec. It's amazing how one's roots call.' Rosemary cleared the trolleys and was very quiet.

CHAPTER FOUR

'I'M sorry about last night,' said Miss Nutford. 'I can't think why she didn't call me. I was off during the afternoon and she knew I planned to stay in and be on call as you had a full day with Sir Tristram.'

'Quite an evening, but I was glad I was there. I hadn't met Dr Hatton and I found that the theatre wasn't as hopeless as I thought. Now that I have a few more gloves and the lotions I ordered, we can cope with most things, and the drums are coming back from Comyns in good shape. I can't think why they didn't do them earlier.'

Miss Nutford poured more tea and handed Rosemary the toast. 'Have you anything today?'

'Mr Moody wants to do something under a local this morning and after that I want to see Miss Dundry to ask her a few things. I heard last night that Mr Nicaise might want to come here after all. At least, he doesn't want to but he has no alternative as every other surgical bed in Bristol seems to be full.'

'You sound as if you object. Don't you like bone surgery?'

'I love it. I've seen a lot in London, but I haven't got over my first meeting with the mighty Mr Nicaise.'

Miss Nutford eyed her curiously. 'He was in the office yesterday. Miss Dundry was trying to persuade him to play bridge.' Rosemary laughed. 'You think that funny? She tries with every new face and is reduced to playing with her old faithfuls.'

'Is that why he came? To talk bridge with the Matron? I thought he was busy at the hospital in the Mendips.'

'He was asking about the staff situation here. He was very interested in the theatre staff in particular.'

'I suppose he wanted to know if he could bring a case here without the patient being killed by our inefficiency,' said Rosemary.

'He seemed much more reasonable, I thought. The last time he came in, he was cross about losing his retractor, as you know, and he said a few choice things about the Birchwood, but now he seems almost anxious to operate here.'

Nick's been talking to him. He's told him that the theatre is under new management and given me a big build up, I suppose, thought Rosemary. Well, he'll have a shock when he discovers that the new theatre sister is the 'half wit' he saw when he stormed into the theatre that evening, and if he recognises me as the dolly girl with the tiny feet who is too frail to walk two hundred yards, he'll have an even bigger shock.

Rosemary yawned.

'When did you get to bed?' Miss Nutford asked. 'I must tell Miss Dundry that you have some time owing to you. Make a note of any time you spend on emergencies and make sure you take it. I know from experience that if you let it go, you'll be working for hours and hours with no recompense.'

'It was two o'clock before I left. I had to do one batch of drums in case we needed them in a hurry. Emergencies have a habit of coming in threes, haven't they? and until the drums are all tight fitting, I mean to see that they are done between each case.'

Rosemary walked slowly to the stairs and up to the theatre. The floor was shining and the department was ready for anything that might come in. There was no trace of the ordered chaos of the previous night and Nurse Adams could hardly believe that there had been a case there. 'We leave it until the morning before clearing,' she said. 'The instruments can soak and the linen can too, but we swab the floor.'

'And what happens if another case comes in?'

Adams shrugged. 'If it's a dirty case, what does it matter? We rinse the instruments and boil them and lay up a fresh trolley. It's no different from having a lot of cases following each other during a list.'

'There's a lot of difference. If the case is one like last night, with streptococci everywhere, the chances are that it could spread infection unless we are scrupulous in our cleaning. A suspect appendix would normally be done at the end of a list when all the clean cases were done so that the place could be thoroughly cleaned and disinfected before anything more came in.'

Rosemary gave instructions about the morning's work and told Adams what to prepare for the minor surgery trolley. She sat at her desk and made a list of drugs and lotions she knew might be wanted, added a generous order for new gloves of all sizes and supplies of new synthetic absorbent suture material that Mr Morris would want to use if he brought more major surgery to the hospital. She picked up the list and went down to Miss Dundry's office at twelve. The matron was arranging flowers in the huge rose bowl on the walnut table in the entrance hall. She smiled when Rosemary came and offered her a rose to smell.

Her smile froze when she saw the list. 'I don't think you realise the economies we have to face in these troubled times, Sister. This is very extravagant. I'm sure you can manage without most of these items.' She read aloud the names of the sutures. 'I've never had these in the hospital, Sister. Sir Tristram has never asked for them and neither has Mr Moody or any of the other surgeons.'

'I think they were requested once by a visiting surgeon and she was very annoyed when they couldn't be produced. She said she would never come here again.'

'You seem to have heard a lot of baseless gossip since you arrived here. The gloves, now . . . perhaps we could keep bigger supplies of them.' She smiled as she crossed out the sutures and ticked the gloves, confident that this would satisfy the young and rather upstart sister.

'I have asked for the very minimum that I need, Matron.' Rosemary saw Miss Dundry wince at being given her title. 'If you can't give me your permission, because it is against the policy of the board of governors perhaps, may I ask the secretary to telephone the drug house for the ones you have ticked and I can give this slip to Mr Moody to take up with the board at the next meeting. Perhaps he could persuade them what is wanted. Would you mind signing the slip, Matron?'

'You wouldn't dare go over my head, Sister!'

'I'm sure I'm not doing that, Matron. If board policy states that we economise on essentials, they should be told how important it is to have the right stock. Mr Moody is quite willing to back us up in this.'

Miss Dundry turned a rather mauve shade under her careful make-up, took the slip and signed it, ticking the request for sutures. If looks could kill, thought Rosemary. 'Take it, this time . . . but I hope that this will be the end of such unreasonable requests, Sister. I thought that you came here ready to learn, but I see that you have a stubborn streak that may well lead you into trouble.'

'I'm sorry if you think that, Miss Dundry. I have the good name of the hospital very close to me and I want to make a success of the theatre work here.' Rosemary smiled, with studied innocence. 'How is Mr Turnball this morning?'

'Mr Turnball?'

'Yes, Miss Dundry, the man who came in last night when you asked me to stay on duty to see to the theatre? You remember?' Miss Dundry looked away. 'Miss Nutford told me to make a note of all time spent here after duty, so I made a note of it with the time and date.' She handed the second note to the matron. 'I also haven't been told when I am to have my day off for this week and it's Friday today.'

'Go off now, if that's all you can think about!'

'I can't go now. We have a minor case for Mr Moody soon, but I should like to be off this afternoon and be free to leave the hospital.'

'Take a day off tomorrow . . . and an extra two hours this afternoon.' Miss Dundry turned away and dropped several carnations on the floor in her agitation.

Rosemary bent to pick them up before the water on the stems marked the pale carpet. As she rose to her feet, she felt a hand on her wrist and was helped up.

She held the white carnations in one hand and her other hand was held firmly in a sinuous grip, the brown fingers nearly engulfing her tiny hand. She felt the world stand still for an instant, poised as she was with the absurd and long-stemmed bouquet in her hand, her lips slightly parted and her cheeks tinged with pink after her encounter with Miss Dundry.

'You?' said Mr Nicaise. He seemed amused but slightly wary. 'You look as if you might attack me . . . again, Nurse.'

'I didn't attack you. It was you who was very rude to me.' She tried to drag her hand away and knew with a sense of shock that it had sat very comfortably with him and didn't really want to be taken away. The tops of the carnations trembled violently. 'Do you mind letting go?' she said. 'These are dripping.'

'So we have here a flower arranger . . .'

'Wrong. Miss Dundry dropped them.'

'A theatre nurse with a temper that doesn't match that exquisite shape.'

'Wrong again. If you must know, Mr Nicaise, I'm the new theatre sister in this . . . what did you call it when you were talking to Nick? "That dump, the Birch-wood"?'

'Were you just the slightest bit ashamed to be connected with this place? Was that why you made no mention of working here when you were with your boy-friend?'

'Of course not. I thought that you would never come here again, having found the place quite beneath your notice, so there was no point in becoming in-volved in any discussion about it.'

'And now you are wrong. I *am* coming here to work. I'm here to make sure there will be a room available so that we can operate on Saturday, or Sunday.'

'You can't!'

'And why not?' The dark brows nearly met in a straight and menacing line. 'Do you take the bookings? I've heard of a new broom, but need you take over the whole hospital?'

'You wouldn't like it here. I know.' She stopped, confused.

'Don't you feel up to it? I rather gathered that the new theatre sister was full of her own importance, or so Miss Dundry said when I spoke to her last night.'

'Of course I'm up to it! I've worked . . . with orthopaedics.' She bit back the name that flew to her lips. If he thinks I know Sir Alec, he'll *really* come here. 'There aren't enough staff . . . and I'll probably have the day off,' she said.

'Both days?'

'Tomorrow is Saturday. You have to admit your patient and prepare him. You can't be ready before Sunday, and I shall take Sunday off,' she said with a synthetic sweet smile. Oh, how had this meeting turned into another session of silly bickering? she wondered. Russell Nicaise was watching her face and an enigmatic smile lurked at the edges of his mouth. She saw the firm line of his jaw and his well-shaped nose and wondered if all the women who loved him also wanted to beat their hands on his chest and hate him a little.

'I shall book the room. What you do is your own affair, but if you leave us to the tender mercies of that fat nurse with the permanent scowl, I shall give this hospital such a bad name that nobody of any repute except for Matron's tame physicians will ever enter these doors.' His voice was silky and low, his eyes like jasper and she shivered at the latent force behind the words.

She thrust the flowers into the vase where they hung over the side like seasick travellers, and almost ran into the office where Miss Fane the secretary sat at her desk. 'I have an urgent chit,' said Rosemary. 'Would you phone it through, now, please? I'd like to wait so that I'm sure they have everything there.'

Miss Fane took the list and smiled. 'Miss Dundry changed her mind about this, did she?' She raised the telephone as Miss Dundry came to the door. She paused with the receiver in her hand.

'Oh, I didn't know you were still here, Sister. I . . . I'll come back, Miss Fane.'

'Please finish the call,' said Rosemary.

The secretary dialled and gave the order. 'They have everything in stock and will send it up by this afternoon.' She raised an eyebrow. 'Everything all right, Sister?'

'Better, now I know those things are coming. We really do need them, you know,' she said, softly. 'Are there any messages for me?' Miss Fane handed her two letters and another pink memo slip. 'Thank you, Miss Fane. I shall be off until seven and come back to check the theatre in case anything has been arranged for the weekend. I could pick up the dispensary and stores from here, if you'll keep them.'

'I'll do that. I think it's just as well to check what comes, personally.' She smiled and Rosemary knew that she understood the problem she had to face in Miss Dundry.

Rosemary hurried to the Annexe, her

head in a whirl of conflicting emotions.
There was the light sensation of victory,
however slight, and the gnawing knowledge that she had spoken childishly to Mr
Nicaise and so alienated him even more.
She shivered as she remembered the
almost caressing menace in his last re-
mark. He looked very taut and his very
quietness was like the peace in the eye of a
storm. If I take one more step out of line, I
shall meet the hurricane, she thought. It
wasn't fair. Sir Alec was coming to Bristol
to do the operation that she knew and
longed to help with again. If Mr Nicaise
asked Matron to take the patient, she
would place every obstacle in the way,
with her desire to keep the hospital for
medical cases.

But isn't that what you want? an inner
voice asked. Haven't you been hoping
that the horrible man will go away and
never be rude to you again?

She opened the pink memo from Nick
and recalled that Mr Nicaise believed that

she and Nick were in love. And that isn't fair either, she thought, illogically.

Nick was leaving for London by an evening train and wouldn't be back for another case for two weeks. 'Meet me for lunch if you can . . . same place at one o'clock,' he'd said.

She flew to change, and decided to wear thonged sandals in which she could walk the streets of Clifton safely without tripping over the cobbles and worn stones. A slim-fitting dress with a petticoat top showed off her soft brown shoulders and the pale coral silk was cool and whispering. She rang through to the theatre and told Nurse Adams that she would be back during the evening for a short while and to go off duty for the evening after telling Miss Nutford she was going.

She knew she had covered the theatre safely, the drugs she had ordered were coming and the drums were no longer a danger, so why wasn't her heart singing?

'You look as if you'd lost a fortune on

the races,' said Nick as he waved from the bar.

'Just tired, I expect. I was up half the night and had a little tussle with Matron this morning.'

'Is that all? Just the ordinary happenings in the everyday life of the average theatre sister.'

'And I met your precious Mr Nicaise again.'

'That must have done something for your ego. I saw the way he eyed your legs last night,' he teased. 'Just as well he wasn't seeing you home.'

She smiled. 'You are an idiot, but you're good for me. I can see why Sue adores you . . . even though we would never suit each other in that way.'

'And you have to do without my protection now. I wish you were five inches taller and had muscle with it.'

'I can look after myself, Nick, but I might be a bit lonely at times. I know very little about this city and until I get a small car, I'm limited to erratic bus time-tables which will probably take me everywhere I *don't* want to go.'

After lunch, they strolled through the hilly streets of the old part of the city above the ancient Gorge and Rosemary knew that if she could be happy in her work, she would enjoy living there. She paused to look in shop windows as they walked back towards the bridge and on an impulse she went into a florist's shop to buy a potted plant to add at least a touch of greenery to her austere room. Nick was buying chocolates to take back to Sue in the shop next door and Rosemary was undecided what to buy. She saw several ornate baskets of fruit bearing tiny labels addressed to the Birchwood Hospital and knew that this was the local branch of the firm that acted as an agency for sending gifts of fruit and flowers to other cities and other countries. She smiled as she thought of the many patients with gastric com-plaints who were tortured by such gifts, unable as they were to eat the delicious fruit and forced to give it away to other patients or to the staff. Life could be very unfair. She selected a fine plant that would grow quickly and fill her window sill with bright green leaves in a short time.

A man with his back towards her was sending flowers. He asked what the cost would be to send them to Canada and pushed a card towards the girl. 'Please ask them to include this message,' he said.

'To remind you of the anniversary. Some people still remember,' she quoted. He nodded, and Rosemary decided that she would come to the shop on another day to buy her plant. She slipped away to the sweet shop and helped Nick to choose the chocolates, hoping that Mr Russell Nicaise would not be sending his . . . lover or wife some chocolates also.

'I thought you wanted to buy a plant,' Nick said.

'It was too crowded in there,' she said.

'What lies behind that road? Have you time to explore?'

They crossed the road and Russell Nicaise watched them go down the narrow side street, before walking in the opposite direction.

The river looked as if a plug had been taken out and the water had run out through the banks of mud. 'No boats today,' said Nick. 'It's a beautiful river when the tide is right so we have to put up with it when it's like this.' They sat on the grass and looked across at the woods that flanked the Gorge. Beyond the trees, Rosemary knew that there were houses built in another era, of charm and elegance, very similar to the houses that made up the Birchwood Hospital and Annexe, but which were now split into units of apartments and maisonettes inside the impressive exteriors. She picked a stem of grass.

'I'll have to bring Sue here. She'll love it,' Nick said.

'It must be lovely at night,' said Rose-mary.

'Promise me you will not come here alone. I wouldn't like to think of you here without a guy to look after you.'

'Does that mean you condemn me to walking round the garden of the Birch-wood and never see the moonlight on the river?' She laughed, but a fluttering of near panic seized her. It could happen. She was very much alone and he was right in thinking she couldn't walk in the dark alone in this place of shadows and trees. 'I shall take a taxi if I'm in the city at night for a concert or when I go to the theatre,' she said. The drained river looked lonely as if all life had gone and nothing was left but dull greyness. Had the time in London when she trained with all her friends and was seldom left alone been the best that life had to offer? Would everything she did now have an element of anticlimax?

'I wish I was going back to London, Nick.'

'I thought you wanted your own theatre. If you stayed at Beatties, you would be restricted to one type of surgery, wouldn't you, until you were a departmental head? I've often thought that you gain more experience once you are well-trained if you come to a well-run nursing home or small hospital where every leading surgeon of the area will bring work of all types.'

'That's what I thought. I've been in most of the theatres during my general training and I didn't want to specialise until I was sure of what kind of work I wanted.'

'Sue said she wanted to be in the heart-lung unit until she had to stand for hours scrubbed and holding a retractor and swab-holder and never really seeing what was being done. In a teaching hospital there are too many people all agog to see what goes on inside the incision.'

'I found that, too. It gets a bit claustrophobic in some ENT theatres too when most of the nose and ear work is done in blacked-out conditions using headlamps and microscopes, but I enjoy that work. The surgeons often get me to tie sutures as my hands are so small.'

'How do you get on with the heavy cases? Take this hip job, for instance. He's a big man, overweight and tall, so he'll be a problem to get on and off the table if you don't have height and muscle.'

'It doesn't follow,' said Rosemary. 'Lifting is a knack that even the smallest nurse can do if she approaches the problem in the right way. I'm more concerned with the operation. Sometimes it's impossible to fit a self-retaining retractor in a hip incision and it all has to be done manually. The surgeon can forget that on the end of a hand-held retractor is a small nurse or sister with a hand that no longer has any feeling.' She frowned in mock seriousness. 'I hope you aren't guilty of that, Mr Tadworth.'

'I am as guilty as the rest. A lot of swine,

aren't we?' he said, with an easy smile.

'Not you, Nick . . . I could name a few, but not you.' Her eyes were suddenly misty. 'I wish I had a brother like you, Nick.'

'Come on, you're getting morbid.' He gave her a bear hug and kissed her cheek, lightly. 'I'll buy you a great big vulgar ice-cream and we can walk across the bridge eating like tourists. I hope you see Miss Dundry . . . or better still that she sees you when she whisks by in her carriage and pair.'

'Carriage and pair?'

'Well, she's behind the times in every other way, why not in her transport?' They laughed, and to the man who watched them from the path leading up to the observatory tower, they were happy and very close.

'I don't have to go back yet,' said Rosemary. 'I want to explore and if I can't come here alone at night, I'll have to do it by day. If you have to go and pack, I can walk up to the top and see the bridge from there. It must be a fine view.'

Nick thrust an enormous ice-cream cone into her hand in spite of her laughing protests and went back to the hotel. She licked the already melting strawberry-flavoured confection and strolled up the winding path that flanked the edge of the Gorge, leading gently up to the top of the cliff from whence she had a spectacular view of the graceful bridge. The sun shone on the incoming tide and gulls swooped screaming over the waste thrown overboard from a boat waiting for the water to deepen and carry it down river. She saw a cave half way down the rock face and turned her back to look up at the circular tower that dominated the rock. She went to read the Victorian notice on the side of the tower and saw that at the top of the tower was a Camera Obscura. She smiled as she made out the message that it was possible to see a wide expanse of Clifton Down, the Suspension Bridge and the surrounding countryside 'to the amazement of the beholder'.

What fun! The door was open and a small group of people stood waiting by a pay kiosk. She finished her cone and joined them, suddenly in a holiday mood. A few people came down the narrow winding stairs including a little boy who screamed that he wanted to go back and see it again, but was dragged away by his mother with the promise of ice-cream. And I'm doing it in reverse, thought Rosemary. I've had my cheering-up treat and now I climb the tower.

The painted wooden doors at the top of the stairs were wide open, letting in daylight between showings. A large saucer-shaped table filled the main part of the small space and everyone edged round it to make room for more as they came up the stairs. The door was shut and then opened again to let in one more before it was firmly bolted to make sure that no light entered from any other source than from the camera obscura. The saucer was illuminated by the outside light and as the sun came from behind a cloud, the picture of the Down and the Bridge came clearly, with tiny figures walking, ant-like across the grass, and mini cars silently crossing the fairy-tale Bridge.

The attendant pulled a lever and the view changed to the base of the tower, bringing it sharply into focus. A dog ran across the field of vision and was as small as a mouse, but everything was real and as if in reach of stretching hands. A buzz of interested amusement went round the circle in the cramped space. A boy wriggled nearer to get a better view and he begged to be given the overhead lever to operate. Rosemary reached up to push it further along towards the boy and another hand fixed itself firmly on her own. It was a hand that she could not see, from an arm that was hidden in darkness, but a strange thrill of affinity spread from her fingertips and made her tremble.

She freed her hand and let the man's hand push the lever along to the boy. It was too dark to make out any but light colours and she thought she saw the flash of white teeth in a dark face before she drew back and let others go forward. I want to get out of here, she thought. How ridiculous to let the touch of an unknown hand give me a cheap thrill! I must be desperate. Her only thought was to get out and away before she had to see who it was that held her hand for that brief moment. She gave a nervous giggle. Just as well if she didn't see or she'd be ashamed. He might be awful, with a peculiar haircut and sweaty jeans. But she had sensed rather than smelled the absolute cleanliness and faint fragrance of expensive aftershave as his shoulder had touched her breast.

The doors opened and she found the same tiresome boy pushing his way out and obstructing the exit. He pushed past her and lumbered down the echoing stairs. Rosemary stumbled in her haste to get to the stairs and once more the hand gripped her arm, bringing her back sharply from an imminent fall. 'You really must look where you are going,' said Mr Russell Nicaise, grinning at her infuriatingly. 'Those tiny feet . . . even in those sandals, seem to lead you into trouble.'

'They serve me very well,' she said, with dignity. 'I was pushed . . . I didn't fall.'

'Well, if you will try to race small boys down dangerous stairs, what can you expect?' He shook his head gravely. 'So undignified . . . almost as undignified as a theatre sister sucking bright pink ice-cream from a soggy cornet.'

'It wasn't soggy . . . it was crisp and delicious.' They were down in the sunlight and the next batch of viewers streamed past them up the stairs. She glanced sideways and saw that he was smiling. 'You saw me with Nick? Why didn't you speak to him?'

'I didn't like to disturb your leave-taking. I know he goes back today and you hadn't a lot of time together.' He lost the brightness from his eyes. 'Nick seems to enjoy life.'

'Nick is wonderful,' she said, simply. It might help if he thought that she was in love with Nick. She saw the brown hand still on her arm and pulled away, finding his touch as disturbing as it had been in the darkness of the tower. I think it's a *very* good idea, she told herself. Life at Birchwood is difficult enough now, it will be even more difficult if he comes to work there and finds fault with everything I do . . . and it would be impossible if I find I'm attracted to him, physically . . . and in spite of my better judgment. He was in love with the woman in Canada to whom he sent expensive flowers . . . for an anniversary. He was in no hurry to leave her and she found that they were walking back towards Clifton.

'I have to get back,' she said. 'I have

to check the theatre and see that some supplies I ordered have come.'

'You have to do that, personally?'

'Of course.' Her tone was cool. 'If I am to run an efficient theatre I have to do most things myself until I know I can delegate, safely.'

'A quart of fire in a pint packet,' he teased, but it was without insult. 'I had no idea that you were so fierce when I met you with Nick, but as soon as I saw you again and remembered our first meeting, I knew that I would have to watch my step.'

'So even the great Mr Nicaise trips up sometimes?' she said, demurely.

'Yes, I should get my facts straight. I'm sorry about the retractor, but it was the final straw to a pretty disastrous session in your theatre.' His mouth set in a hard line.

'It wasn't *my* theatre then and surely Miss Nutford was efficient?'

'She was called away at a vital point and

I was left to the tender mercies of the nurse who looks as if she would like to throw all surgeons into the pit. I wonder she stays if she dislikes it all so much.'

'She liked it when there were very few cases that took much effort, like those Sir Tristram brings in.'

'Well, she's in for a shock! I operate on Sunday.'

He glanced sideways, waiting for her reaction.

So this is why he is walking with me and being pleasant, she decided.

'I saw Matron and she agreed that Sir Alec should have the theatre on Sunday and that you would be there to run things.'

'I see. You will bring your instruments in good time, I hope?' She was crisp and business-like. 'Perhaps you will make a list of anything that Sir Alec is likely to need.'

He flushed. 'I expect he will tell you when he comes. I am hoping to do most of the operation, but I can't be expected to know about his preferences.'

'You leave all that to the theatre sister,' she said, sweetly. 'You expect me to know even if you suspect that I have never seen a case like it!'

'I'm sure you'll manage . . . if only to talk your way out of anything that you find awkward.' He saw her rising anger. 'Now, if we are to work together, let's start again, shall we?' His smile was so sweet that her heart ached and she wanted to put her hand back into the protective warmth of his firm fingers again.

'Fine.' She looked at her watch.

'No, it isn't late. You are off until seven.'

'How did you know?'

'I heard it said . . . on the grapevine.' He tucked her hand in his arm and walked briskly. 'I'll buy you a cup of tea, you can go back and check your theatre and then I suggest a professional consultation about this case, while we have a meal, unless you are joining Nick in town for your day off?'

He waited for her reply as if it was important.

'No, Nick will be too busy to see me again this weekend,' she said. 'I have arranged to meet a friend, tomorrow,' she lied.

'Come on, we'll find some tea and I shall drive you back to the Birchwood.'

He wants to make a good impression on Sir Alec, and can't do that if he is at odds with the theatre sister, she thought. But the sun was shining, he wanted some tea and when he was as charming as he could be on occasion, why not enjoy his company even if he was engaged . . . or married to the woman in Canada?

'I suppose you speak French,' she said.

'Yes . . . why do you ask? Oh, I suppose the name . . . we come from Normandy and I have connections in Britain and French Canada.'

'Is your French as perfect as your English?'

'Pretty good, I think.' He grinned. 'English is good for all things professional . . . but they say that French is a better language for making love.'

'I wouldn't know,' she said, through dry lips.

CHAPTER FIVE

'Oн, it's you, Mr Moody. I wondered who had left the lights on.'

'Can I borrow a pair of sterile gloves, Sister. The man we did last night is doing well, but I want to keep clean when I look under his dressing because I am going on to look at some clean cases afterwards.'

Sister Rosemary Clare smiled. 'I wish everyone was as careful in this place,' she said, and placed a pack of number eight gloves inside a sterile towel so that he could carry it down to the wing. 'No problems? I asked Miss Dundry how he was this morning, but I doubt if she had seen him.'

'I think he'll make an uneventful recovery in spite of not having antibiotics pumped into him. His drip is finished and he's taking fluids by mouth with no sickness. Bruce Hatton is a genius. He keeps his patients light and yet relaxed and we seldom have trouble with vomiting after they come round.'

'I was very impressed. I think he's coming for an important orthopaedic case on Sunday.'

'On Sunday? I thought it was taboo to come here for anything more than visiting and the odd game of Bridge on Sunday!' He grinned. 'Who is doing it?'

'Sir Alec Perivale is coming and his assistant, who will be doing most of it, is to be Mr Russell Nicaise. Do you know him?'

'I haven't met him yet, but I want to do so. I have a case in the country that worried me last week when I first saw him. He has a badly swollen leg that hasn't responded to antibiotics and his temperature fluctuates between sub-normal and high. I thought it was an abscess at first, but hesitated to drain it. I now think it may be osteomyelitis and rather out of my range.'

He picked up the pack. 'You don't know his phone number do you, Sister? There's nobody in the office downstairs and I want to contact him as soon as possible. We ought to have him admitted,' he muttered.

'He will be here this evening, Mr Moody. He wants to talk over the case we are doing on Sunday.'

'When is he coming here? Are you going to be on duty for much longer, Sister?'

'No, I'm off soon and I have a day off tomorrow,' she said, to leave him in no doubt that if he wanted the theatre opened it would be under the care of Miss Nutford and not the new sister. 'Is this a private case?' She put the last of the new batch of stores away, having noted with satisfaction that everything she had ordered was there. 'Mr Nicaise is coming here at eight-thirty,' she said.

'Good . . . I wonder if he will have eaten by then? I'd like to talk to him and take him to see the boy if it was possible.' He saw her sudden confusion. 'What is it, Sister?'

'He said he would take me out for a meal,' she said, and blushed.

'Oh, I say . . . that was quick.' He laughed. 'I might have known you'd ensnare every likely male for miles.'

'It isn't like that. He wants to discuss the case and he's a friend of a good friend of mine from my training school.' It sounded weak, but Clive Moody nodded. 'I have no need to go out with him tonight if you want to talk shop,' she said. 'I know more or less what is required for Sunday and now that I have more confidence in the asepsis here, I feel confident that we can cope with whatever comes in, given due warning,' she added.

'Perhaps you'd introduce me to him and we'll take it from there, but I wouldn't dream of taking him away. You must eat . . . we could all eat together if, as you say, this is a purely professional arrangement.'

She smiled. It would be a relief. The thought of being with Russell Nicaise for an entire evening in the intimate surroundings of a dimly lit restaurant was unnerving to say the least. The fact that he would be thinking of his love in Canada would make it no easier to be with him, now that she admitted to herself that she was physically attracted to the half-French and very good-looking man.

Mr Moody sat in the surgeons' room and read some medical journals, made a couple of telephone calls and waited for her to go off duty.

'I'll be back in the foyer at eight-twenty,' she said, and rushed over to the annexe. I'm suddenly in demand, tonight! Even if it is my expertise they want and not my body, it's good to be needed! and she warmed to the pleasant surgeon who knew his own limitations and didn't mind passing on a case to someone who knew more about the condition than he did.

She dressed in a soft cotton jump suit with a dusky green abstract print and took a large shawl as a cover up if the evening turned cool. The air was warm under a softly starlit sky and she hurried down to the entrance of the annexe, ready to meet Russell Nicaise. She started as his tall figure appeared in the doorway. 'I thought we were to meet at the Birchwood,' she said.

'I was early,' he said, shortly. 'I went to have a close look at the bridge again. It's lit up tonight. Come and see it.'

'First, there's someone you should meet. Mr Moody, one of the general surgeons, was asking for you. I couldn't give him your phone number so he waited to see you.'

'Damn!' he said, clearly.

'I'm sorry . . . I didn't think you'd mind, and what could I do?'

He glanced at her in exasperation. 'I like to be off duty sometimes,' he said.

'But you aren't . . . I mean, we are going to talk shop, so why not include him? He suggested that we all ate together.'

'Oh, he did, did he? I like to choose my own dinner companions.'

'Well, you can tell him. He's waiting over there.' She hurried forward and called Clive Moody. 'This is Mr Nicaise,' she said. 'I haven't had the pleasure of seeing him operate yet, but his fame has come before him.' She gave him a smile of mocking sweetness and stood back.

'Just the man I want to see.' Clive Moody went straight into details about the sick boy and Rosemary saw Russell Nicaise relax, his interest growing. 'I'd like you to see him soon . . . tomorrow if possible. His family want him treated privately but there is a snag. He's petrified of hospitals after a bad session following a road accident and they wanted him examined in his own home.'

'Where does he live?'

'Out of town, I'm afraid. On the road to Priddy in the Mendips. If we could get him there, they have a bed in the orthopaedic hospital there, but I fancy he would be more co-operative in a place like this that looks rather like a private house and doesn't reek of disinfectants.'

'Can we eat out there? What if we eat together after we've seen him?' Russell Nicaise smiled, slyly, as if it was all his own idea to eat together. 'We can combine business with pleasure . . . if you can bring yourself to put up with two boring surgeons instead of one, Sister.'

'That's great. I'll pop back and telephone the family, and put a call through to a very nice little pub near one of the lakes,' Clive Moody was enthusiastic.

'What a good idea of yours, Mr Nicaise,' said Rosemary, caustically. 'I shall enjoy having dinner with you . . .

and Mr Moody, unless you would rather I stayed here. I can't imagine what there is to discuss about the case, if you can't tell me what Sir Alec likes his theatre sister to prepare. I do have a lot to unpack and I need to have a good night's sleep.'

'You've all day tomorrow to do that and rest and be fresh and bushy-tailed for the case on Sunday.' He looked down at her feet. 'More new shoes? I hope that Moody's patient doesn't live across a ploughed field.' She tried to appear un-moved by his teasing and by the apprais-ing glance he gave her. 'You could go by helicopter or . . . hot-air balloon in that fetching flying suit.'

'I'm beginning to be very glad that Mr Moody is coming with us. Do you make personal remarks to every female who crosses your path?'

'Only pretty ones,' he said, and the jasper eyes glowed like living coals.

'I thought it was a general stock in trade that you use on patients and the staff alike. I hope you remember to compliment my theatre nurse . . . it would make more impact on her than on me.'

'Can't you take a sincere compliment?' His face hardened.

'Let's say I don't like men who pay compliments to women when they're away from their girlfriends.'

'You mean that Nick never pays another girl a compliment? Not even when he is in London, surrounded by lovely nurses?'

'That's different . . . Nick and I understand each other and we would never get a false impresssion.'

'How very civilised.' He raised one eyebrow. 'But there is nothing in the book of rules to forbid me from saying that you are pretty . . . that you have a lovely body and that when you are angry, the glow of those green eyes could make a man mad.' He stepped forward and took her into a close embrace. It happened so quickly that she was limp in his arms as he kissed her, fiercely, bruising her lips, before putting her back on her feet again. Only then did she know that she had been held up like a doll, with her small feet beating the air.

'Oh . . . you beast! I suppose just because you are far away from your girlfriend, you think any woman is fair game. I hate you, Mr Nicaise!'

'A positive emotion at last,' he said, calmly. 'Moody is just coming out of the front hall, so shall we forgive and forget?' His lips twitched and his eyes were wicked and triumphant. 'You can't very well say I attacked you . . . that blush suits you very well.'

'Don't ever do that again,' she said and went to meet Clive Moody. 'I don't think I need to come with you,' she said. 'Mr Nicaise and I have had . . . a little chat and understand each other. I know exactly what will be needed for the case on Sunday, so you can feel free to talk shop all night if you like . . . without me.'

'Rubbish,' he said, firmly and took her arm. 'I've booked a table and I'm looking forward to a very pleasant meal. It's time we got to know each other, eh, Nicaise?'

'Oh, I do so agree,' he said, solemnly. 'And while we are getting to know one another . . . my name is Russell. And you, Sister?' he asked politely, the laughter hidden under hooded lids.

'Rosemary,' she said, reluctantly.

'And from now on, I'm Clive. That puts us on a good basis for the future. I can't tell you what a difference you have made already, Rosemary. Don't you agree, Russell?'

'He hasn't seen me in action yet,' she said. 'Some of the staff still think I must be a mindless idiot or a tiny dolly bird with no competence, so I'd rather not hear polite platitudes until I can prove that I am a good theatre sister.'

'That puts you firmly in your place, Russell,' laughed Clive Moody. 'How shall we go? My car, I think as it has a better back seat than your fast-back. I also claim the privilege as driver, of having the lady in the passenger seat.'

Rosemary breathed more easily. It would have been impossible to sit with Russell Nicaise and feel the contact of his arm against her own and the brush of his hand on her thigh in the confined space of his two-seater sports car. It was almost impossible to allow him to hand her into the car, but she had no alternative to permitting what seemed a detached and polite gesture. He's a rake, she fumed to herself. He has a girlfriend . . . probably a wife in Canada, and he thinks that Nick and I have something going, but he tried to force me to succumb to his great attraction. He was like many handsome doctors, who walked the corridors of healing and took it for granted that every nurse and female medical student would fall madly in love with them.

'I'll take you the pretty way,' said Clive. 'I'd like to go straight to the farm where the boy lives and have your opinion, and when we have decided what to do about him, we can all relax and enjoy the rest of the evening.' He hummed softly as he drove, enjoying the drive and the company and the sensation of relief that Russell Nicaise would help him in a difficult decision.

They found the farm at the end of a winding lane, deep in the soft Mendip hills. Outcrops of grey stone broke up the field on the edge of a stream and glimpses of yellow gorse lit the hedges. The air was soft and pure and Rosemary took a deep breath as she left the car. 'I'll wait for you,' she said. 'This is a lovely place. I'd like to sit and admire the view.'

The two men strode away to the wide door of the farmhouse and after a few moments, disappeared inside. Lights shone from many windows and Rosemary could see figures against the uncurtained windows as dusk threw them into relief. She walked to a low wall and sat on it, the

warm breeze lifting tendrils of her soft
hair and caressing her cheeks. She almost
laughed. What was she doing there? She
was with two men whom she hardly knew,
one who she respected as a surgeon and
liked as a pleasant and good-tempered
man . . . married, with two children but
enjoying the company of a pretty girl. The
other? I shall never know him. I shall
never be able to get close to him. Any
contact we make contains something
dangerous . . . she shivered as she re-
called the frisson of sensual awareness
that she unwillingly admitted existed
when he touched her hand and helped her
into the car. The fierce, bold kiss had
infuriated her, but it had awakened feelings that she had only suspected herself
capable of possessing when she had believed that the love of her life was Max.

Max . . . she had loved Max with the
breathless delight of a kitten, but this man
with the dark brooding eyes and fine
head, stirred her to thoughts of which she

was ashamed. She walked to the stream and tried to dismiss him from her mind. He was no good. He had a woman somewhere to whom he sent flowers and messages about an anniversary and he had no right to make love to another girl. It would serve him right if I told him that Nick was engaged to Sue and let him think I was fair game . . . if I could make him want me enough to hurt him when he saw that I was only playing. She blushed in the moth-filled dusk. He did want me. The mercurial flow of desire had been there between them, and it had not been flowing one way only.

She waited until the door opened and a rectangle of golden light silhouetted the figures of the two men and the parents of the child. Rosemary went quietly back to the car and sat in the passenger seat.

'I hope we didn't bore you?'

'I enjoyed watching the trees against the fantastic sky,' she said.

'Good. We can have dinner now. Russell is taking him into the orthopaedic unit tomorrow. Michael said he doesn't mind going to hospital if he knows who he will see there, and he seemed to like you, Russell.'

'Of course,' said Russell Nicaise. 'It helps a lot to see a friendly face that has appeared in familiar surroundings. I approve of domiciliary visits in cases like this.' He laughed. 'And of course . . . to know me is to love me, isn't it, Rosemary?'

'Not necessarily,' she said, coolly, 'and if you bring many cases into the Birchwood on Sundays, you will be very unpopular with the people who matter.'

'Such as?'

'Miss Dundry, who likes to give sherry before Sunday lunch to Sir Tristram and his wife and some of the other regulars. It isn't seemly to have people rushing about with theatre trolleys and gowns.'

'And how do you react, Rosemary?' said Clive Moody. 'I never book at weekends if I can avoid it, but there is sometimes an emergency. I treasure my weekends with the family too much to want to work on Sundays.'

'Emergencies are fine. That's what acute surgery is all about, if I have enough staff and equipment to cope safely. I must have some time during the week to get the theatre really clean, but apart from that, it doesn't matter what comes in.'

'You sound confident,' said Russell Nicaise, with a slightly mocking air.

'I know that I can run a good theatre given the chance,' she said, firmly. They stopped at an old coaching inn overlooking one of the lakes and went straight in to eat. The sunset had left streaks of gold above the hills and the lake caught echoes of it in the glinting wavelets. The picture window put into the new dining room to increase the dining area framed a peaceful but slowly disappearing scene and Rosemary sighed. 'It must be beautiful earlier in the evening,' she said. 'When I get a car, I shall come and picnic here.'

'I shall certainly make a point of doing that,' said Russell Nicaise.

She glanced at him, sharply but his eyes were expressionless. He doesn't mean that he wants to come with me, she thought. You're being silly, reading more into one kiss than was ever intended. He can't be all bad if that child liked him.

'Is . . . Michael . . . did you say? Is he very ill?'

'It's almost definitely an abscess in the tibia. We'll have to open it and drain it and then he should respond to the usual treatments. When he was involved with the car accident, he must have injured the bone and nobody noticed with all the rest of the bruising. It probably subsided, but when the surface wounds healed, infection was left deep inside and infected the bone. He's young and healthy and should be riding his pony again in a month.'

'That's enough shop talk. If anyone faints and they call for a doctor . . . I'm off duty,' said Clive, firmly. 'I intend ordering a large carafe of the house wine which is very good. You'll have to drink most of it if I'm driving, but it's a very pleasant wine.'

They ordered deep-fried mushrooms and discovered that they all liked the French food on the menu. Rosemary helped herself to crisp salad to go with salmon in a perfect sauce and began to enjoy herself as she had not done for weeks. Clive was good company and had a fund of very good anecdotes to tell, about his family, his early days as a student and the travels he enjoyed when he was un-encumbered by a rising family. 'I went across America with two friends,' he said. 'We ran out of money and couldn't do more than touch the fringes of Canada. We saw Niagara of course, from both sides of the falls, and we visited friends in Toronto. We didn't hit Quebec. Isn't that where you have connections, Russell?'

'Yes, I have many friends there and

some of my family go there even now. I shall have to go there soon, but I'm not looking forward to it as most of my family live in Europe and I've got into the habit of meeting them in England.'

'Are you going to work there?' said Clive.

'I shall look in at the unit where I did some work, watch a few new procedures, and they've asked me to demonstrate the one we perfected in London.' He turned to Rosemary. 'That's why I want to do this one on Sunday. If I have flown solo, so to speak, I shall be able to cope in Canada.' He looked at her over the top of his wine glass, and his eyes burned with a sombre light. 'What I really need is a good assistant . . . or theatre sister to hold my hand.'

'You should ask Sir Alec Perivale. Just the man to suggest someone efficient. He hates fools and would never recommend anyone he wasn't happy about,' said Rosemary.

'How do you know?'

'His fame comes before him,' she said, quickly. 'Nick was talking about him.' She spooned up the last of her profiteroles. 'I'm looking forward to seeing him.' Her grey-green eyes gave away nothing of her thoughts. Let it be a nice surprise. Let Mr Know-all Nicaise think he can tell me what to do on Sunday and then discover that Sir Alec and I work together like a dream.

'Ah, yes; Nick. How long have you known him?' She sensed the curiosity of the two men.

'Is he the man I saw you with the other day?' said Clive.

'Bristol has half a million people and you have to see me with one man,' she said, lightly. 'I've known Nick for ages.'

'He isn't going to whisk you away just as you get used to us and seem to be rejuvenating the Birchwood, is he?' said Clive.

'No, he isn't likely to do that,' she said.

'We both have work to do.' And he can make of that what he likes, she thought, seeing the dark eyes looking pensive.

They drank coffee overlooking a small path along which night fishermen walked, during the season for trout. The conversation turned to fishing and foreign travel and Rosemary hoped that she would hear something about the background of the man who had such a distracting effect on her heart. He told them that he grew up in France, the son of a French father and an English mother. He had lived in French Canada for a while and when his father died, he lived with his mother in England, but visited relatives in Canada and France often enough to make him bi-lingual.

'What was it, Russell? A coronary?' asked Clive, quietly.

'My father? No.' He traced a pattern with the end of a spoon on the table cover. 'He was killed while inspecting a bridge in Canada. He was a civil engineer and was hoping to build something like the Brunel bridge here, in Canada, to replace a crumbling stone bridge.' He moved restlessly. 'He had wealthy backing and it would have made the area a great tourist attraction as the bridge was to span a gorge similar to this one . . . it was a folly, in a way. I think it was a whim of one wealthy man and a dreamer who was also an engineer.' His face was hard. 'He was a good man and a fine father. The old bridge lay under the first link they threw across the gorge. He went out to the first platform and the cable snapped. He fell on the old bridge instead of in the river and was killed.'

Clive sighed. 'I wonder that you can bear to see the Brunel bridge.'

'On the contrary. It was many years ago and I remember very little of my father, but I shall never forget certain things he said or did that influenced me a lot. I love the Brunel bridge and the other wonderful creations that Brunel achieved. Have you seen the railway station?'

'The station? What has that to do with it?' said Rosemary.

'You need educating, doesn't she, Clive? The station at Temple Meads was designed by the same man. I suppose you'll say next that you have never heard of the SS *Great Britain*, the first iron ship, made from the design of . . .'

'Isambard Kingdom Brunel,' finished Clive with a smile.

'Was that his name? And I have heard of the ship. In fact, I have promised myself a visit to see it as soon as possible. Perhaps tomorrow,' she added, softly.

'If your friend wishes to go there,' said Russell.

'My friend?'

'You said you were spending the day with a friend.'

'Oh, yes . . . not all the day, but some of it,' she said. She smiled, feeling safe now that she knew he would be busy in the hospital in the Mendips. There would be no need to be startled when any man with broad shoulders and dark thick hair came across her path. He would be away and she could explore Bristol with no thought of him . . . or no willing thought.

The car lights stabbed the black silk night. Even the stars were dim behind light cloud and the moon was very new. Moths dashed against the windscreen and the tree shapes bent down over the country lanes with outflung arms. Rosemary sat back, enjoying the smooth motion of the car and wished that life could be like that . . . smooth and uncomplicated, with a hint of beauty and promise around her, even if it was hidden in the dark.

The lights of the Birchwood were soft and the whole place exuded an air of calm comfort. If only her personal relations with the matron were better and she could have more co-operation, life could be very good there.

Clive Moody drew up at the entrance. 'Will this do for you, too, Russell?

Thanks a lot for seeing Michael. I'll ring the hospital and alert them and I'll ring you in the morning with times for surgery.'

'This will do, Clive. I'll escort Rosemary to her door. See you tomorrow.'

'Thank you for taking me,' said Rosemary. She turned to the road again, in the direction of the annexe. 'There's no need for you to come,' she said. 'It's well lit and it isn't far. Goodnight . . . I'll see you on Sunday.' He stood still and she couldn't just turn her back before he made some comment. 'By the way, can I have the instruments in good time? I shall want to lay up carefully, and to be able to tell my nurses what is expected.'

'We hope to make an early start . . . will eight-thirty be too soon?'

'Much too soon! The staff who live out can't come in as early as that on a Sunday.'

'Nine then, at the latest. Perivale is staying overnight in Bristol and wants to

get away back to London as soon as possible.'

'That doesn't give me time to sort out
his cases and sterilise the instruments before he comes.' She hesitated. 'I could go
back for half an hour the night before to
put everything ready and just have the
sterilising to do before he comes.' She
smiled. 'That would be best.'

He still made no move either to go with
her or to move away. 'Could you make
sure I have the cases overnight? Or is he
likely to come in with them when he sees
the patient?'

'I'll bring them, but it might be late.'

'Perhaps you could ring me when you
come? If I'm not in the theatre, ring and
I'll come over. I might be out for the
evening and I would rather leave it until
after ten o'clock, in case I go to a concert.'

'Come and see the bridge,' he said. 'It's
illuminated tonight.' She could see the
glow through the trees and she hesitated.
'Come along,' he said, with a note of

authority. 'Unless you're afraid . . . of the dark . . . or bogey men.'

'I'm not afraid, but I am tired.'

'You must see it,' he said. There was a tension about him that she couldn't understand. It had nothing to do with her, and nothing to do with the kiss he had forced on her earlier. 'I have to see it today, lit up as if for a birthday . . . or a death. Come with me.'

As if in a dream, she let him take her hand and lead her to the road. They trod on early cones from the drying trees and soft grass of the verges. He walked quickly and she was glad to be wearing moccasin shoes that were safe for walking in the dark. A burst of light greeted them as they cleared the trees at the end of the road and the full glory of the delicate-looking bridge took her breath away. It hung like a double row of diamonds against the velvet sky, and the passing traffic in a continuous stream across the roadway was almost hidden, leaving the illusion of two strings of light with no substance beneath them. He still held her hand and she was aware of the tense strong fingers probing her palm.

'It's beautiful,' she said, and stood with him a little above and to the side while the distant hum of the city came up and through the Gorge.

'He was a wonderful man,' said Russell Nicaise. 'There will never be another like him for me.'

'He certainly was a genius who caught the imagination of the public,' she said, slightly surprised at the reaction of this very strong man to the memory of a man who had died a hundred years earlier. She shrugged. I could understand him being devoted to the memory of Lister or Fleming . . . someone to do with medicine, but I suppose even intelligent men like he can get a kind of hero worship for someone with a special skill. A kind of James Dean fantasy, she thought, and smiled.

'Oh . . . yes . . . Brunel was a genius,'

he said, and the tension slipped. She had the impression that they were talking about two different people.

'He *did* build this bridge?'

'Of course . . . and the *Great Britain*.' He linked her hand in his arm and started back. They walked in silence and she wondered at his changing moods. He's European . . . volatile and possibly temperamental. Even Miss Nutford had laughed and said they must make allowances for genius. She wanted to break away but had no intention of struggling with him and his grip was firm on her hand. They reached the doorway to the annexe and she smiled.

'Thank you for coming to see the bridge with me,' he said, seriously.

'It was worth seeing,' she said.

He raised her face to look up into his own and she saw the dark eyes soften and seem to devour her as they sought something in her gaze. She refused to meet his intensity and as his lips closed over hers, she was once more helpless, hypnotised and suddenly afraid of her own feelings. She wanted to reach up and bring his dark head down further to rest on her breast . . . to touch the unruly locks and to savour his kisses and the sweetness of his arms, but she saw in her mind a card that was to go with a bouquet of flowers, to a woman across the sea.

With a sudden movement, she twisted free. 'That is not included in the evening's entertainment,' she said, breathlessly. 'That is not possible between us . . . you should know that.'

'Then you've no right to look like that,' he said, his eyes flashing with what could be guilt . . . or hurt pride.

'Goodnight,' she said, and ran into the annexe. 'I'll see you on Sunday, Mr Nicaise.'

CHAPTER SIX

'You look as if you should be off duty, Sister.' Bruce Hatton, the anaesthetist pushed his heavy case into the anaesthetic room and flexed his hand. 'That case gets heavier every time I use it. If I collect any more gear, I'll need another one.' He looked round the surgeons' room in which were laid out the gowns and masks needed for anyone watching an operation, the rubber boots for the surgeon, his assistant and the anaesthetist, and the tray ready with coffee cups and sugar bowl.

'Expecting a case now?' he said, glancing at his watch.

'No, Dr Hatton. I offered to come in tonight after my day off to get as much ready as possible for the hip case tomorrow morning.' She smiled. 'Evidently you had the same idea. It's an early start if he's to be on the table by nine.'

'A bit mind-shattering on a Sunday, but I believe that Sir Alec has to get back to London. I like to be ready.' He looked at her with approval. 'It's good to have someone here who cares, Sister. Have you seen one of these done?'

'I've scrubbed for Sir Alec many times and know this new procedure very well.'

'I'll bet Nicaise is glad to have you here, in that case.'

'He doesn't yet know that I've even seen this op. I thought it would be a nice surprise,' she said, demurely.

'Taking one arrogant Frenchman down to size, are you?' He chuckled. 'I shall enjoy seeing that.' He frowned. 'That was unfair. The arrogant bit was my first impression, but I have met him since then and found him very sound.'

'Let's hope I do, too,' she said. 'Now that you're here, tell me if there's anything special you like in the way of lubricants or lotions, cutting-down sets or whatever might be needed.'

'This *is* something new! I've been in the habit of bringing everything I can think I'd need.' She unlocked a small cupboard in the anaesthetic room. 'That's very good,' he said. 'If you are as efficient in the main theatre as you are here, we could do all our major private surgery here.'

'Please ask if you find something missing. I can't promise miracles at once, but I think we're winning,' she said, with a smile. She unlocked the bigger of the two cases left by Sir Alec and saw again the familiar instruments that accompanied him on all his visits out of London. Deftly, she separated them into the batches she knew he liked to have on separate trolleys and made sure that there was plenty of the suture material ready in sterile packs. She checked the glove drums and carefully wrapped the spare metal heads and sockets that might be needed as hip replacements if the ones in the drums were unsuitable and a more conventional method had to be used. She used soft old towels for the wrappings so that if the steriliser was boiling fast, there was no possibility of any scratches appearing on the polished surfaces.

Bruce Hatton watched and his eyes missed nothing. He saw the easy proficiency and the care, the spotless theatre and the shining sterilisers which looked almost new after a protracted cleaning session that had made Nurse Adams mutter under her breath about fussy little bitches. 'Don't stay too long,' he said. 'It might be quite a morning. Get some rest.'

'Done now,' she said. 'I can't do any more even if I wanted to.' She closed the second case and put them both neatly in her office. 'If you're ready to go, Dr Hatton, I'll put out the lights.'

It was midnight and she was looking forward to a deep bath, a good sleep and a satisfying but perhaps tiring morning. The telephone rang and Miss Dundry gasped with relief. 'I saw the lights on and wondered if you were there, Sister.' She seemed quite unconcerned that the new theatre sister was in the theatre at midnight on her day off. 'Mr Snelgrove is here with a patient. He insists that an operation is necessary tonight.'

'But that's impossible, Matron. I've been preparing for a clean surgical case for tomorrow . . . you know, the hip case for Sir Alec.'

'I'm very sorry, Sister, but there is no alternative. If I'd known that you were back in the hospital I could have told you earlier.'

'You mean that the patient was admitted some time ago? You let me lay up for tomorrow before telling me there was a dirty case coming here? When was the patient admitted?' Anger made her bold. 'If it was before the day staff left, they could have coped and still made the theatre clean for tomorrow.'

'Really, Sister! Your job is to see that

the theatre is fit for use at any time of the day or night and not to question my decisions.'

Dr Hatton saw the angry incredulity in the girl's eyes and took the receiver from her. 'Dr Hatton here, Matron. I'd like more details about this case. When was he admitted?' His crisp voice brooked no argument. Rosemary saw his mouth tighten. 'Seven o'clock . . . and I take it that Mr Snelgrove was not anxious about the patient at that time?' He listened again. 'In fact, Matron, you admitted the patient here on condition that Mr Snelgrove waited until Sister Clare was back in the building before he used the theatre?'

Rosemary gasped. 'But Miss Nutford takes emergencies if I'm off and there was no certainty of my being here tonight. If I'd arranged to sleep out, I'm not officially on duty until the morning,' she said in a hurried whisper.

'And the man is worse?' The line crackled. 'Oh, is that you, Snelgrove. What the hell are you and Matron playing at? Sister Clare is off duty but had come back to get the theatre ready for a very important case early tomorrow.' A man's voice sounded high and apologetic and Dr Hatton nodded. 'I see. I'll stay and give the anaesthetic . . . and tell Matron that I shall want two nurses here to help Sister and me . . . yes, two. They will stay until the theatre is spotless once more after the case has gone back to the ward and if Sister doesn't have full co-operation, I shall raise this with the board of governors at the next meeting. Please tell her.'

'Thank you,' said Rosemary. 'What is it, Dr Hatton?'

'The X-rays showed an abscess that needs draining and there is a danger of septicaemia. He had his gall bladder removed some time ago but had never been really fit. Temperature fluctuating . . . tenderness, all the local signs of something there.' He looked grim. 'Let's hope it isn't a swab left inside!'

Rosemary bit her lip and flew to put the general set on to boil. She had everything ready by the time the man was unconscious on the table and a rather chastened Mr Snelgrove made the incision. A minute later, a flood of foul discharge flowed from the wound and the dirty nurse was kept busy placing soiled swabs in lines for checking. The wound was washed out and insufflated with antibiotics and a wide drain sewn in to ensure that it didn't heal completely until all discharge had gone and the patient's temperature was normal once more.

Rosemary applied the dressing and pulled the blanket over the patient's chest. Two nurses from the ward came to take the trolley down and Dr Hatton went with them. 'I would like some coffee, if it's not too much trouble, Sister. I want to see Night Sister about the pre-medication tomorrow and I'll check on Mr Soames as soon as he's back in bed. I'll tell them to put him in a high Fowler's position as soon as he's out of anaesthetic to drain that stuff into a bottle, and then I'll come back here.'

The theatre looked as if a tornado had hit it. The smell of the septic discharge pervaded the atmosphere and the nurse who gathered up the dirty dressings had to seal them into a large plastic pack before they went down the shute to the incinerator. The sluiced towels went down in a bag marked 'very dirty' and gradually the main theatre resumed its now usual appearance of clean efficiency. The house telephone rang and the sister from the ward asked if her nurses could come back, but Rosemary firmly repeated Dr Hatton's promise that they must stay until everything was clear. 'If you need a nurse, I'm afraid you must take the matter up with Matron,' she said, firmly. And I hope they have a blazing row about it, she thought as she scrubbed the instruments. The welcome smell of disinfectant fol-lowed the sweeps of the wet mop used on the floor and the walls shone after being washed down with more disinfectant. One of the nurses grumbled, but Rosemary told her about the bone surgery booked for the morning and explained the importance of a clean theatre.

Dr Hatton came back and insisted that Sister Clare should join him over a coffee pot and she discovered that she was ready for a little stimulant. They munched biscuits too when they had thanked the night staff for their help and decided that nothing further could be done until the morning. 'Four o'clock . . . and we're back where we were at midnight, Sister. Do you think you can cope with tomorrow . . . or rather, today.'

'I shall be all right once we've started, Dr Hatton.' She gave a weary smile. 'The work doesn't necessarily worry me, but in a place like this with limited staff, there should be firm rules about the use of the theatre. It just isn't safe to mix dirty and clean cases unless we have more staff to clean up in between. I'm very grateful for your support. I sometimes wonder if it's worth staying here.'

'May I quote you on that?'

'Where would that be?'

'At the next meeting. Several of us have grumbled behind our hands for long enough. Now that we have a good sister, it's up to us to get some changes here. I shall make sure that not only the Bridge crowd attend the next meeting, but all of the interested surgeons. We have been invited to attend in the past, but I think it was only a courtesy and neither Matron nor her old friends really expected us to come, let alone insist on changes.' He smiled. 'My wife will think I've deserted her. I rang through and told her I would be sleeping in the annexe yet again. It's not a bad idea. I sleep there and walk briskly across the bridge for breakfast and feel relatively fresh for a case if there's an early one.'

'Goodnight, Dr Hatton, and thank

you,' said Rosemary. She watched him go and made a quick check again before putting out the lights and going across to the annexe. Half past four in the morning and she must be up at six-thirty, to dress, have breakfast, put on the instruments . . . no, I'll do that before breakfast, and eat while they boil. I ought to leave a note for early breakfast . . . It was nearer dawn, she thought, and it was five before she clambered into bed and sank into a fitful sleep. I must be ready to cope, was her last thought before sleeping. What will Russell Nicaise have to say if I appear limp and with sluggish reactions?

She heard the distant traffic from the bridge and the distant siren of a police car. The city was never really asleep, and the night sounds merged with day, bringing milk floats and delivery vans to disturb her and force her tightly shut eyes to open. She groped for her watch and sprang out of bed. There was just time for a shower to freshen her and the cool water shocked her into wakefulness.

The theatre smelled fresh and she thrust away the nightmare that had haunted her sleep, of arriving to find Nurse Adams picking up dirty swabs from a filthy floor. The sterilisers bubbled and Nurse Price came in early as she had promised, and checked the unsterile trolleys with assurance, adding to the good impression she had already made on the new sister. They went down to breakfast and Nurse Adams joined them on the way back, full of toast and ill-concealed curiosity about the night's work.

Rosemary said little, stressing that they had more important matters to think of and then told her exactly what was expected of her during the case. Even Nurse Adams liked to know what to do and was showing signs of enjoying being a part of a good team. Rosemary felt her spirits rise as the time drew near for the patient to come up in the lift, and Dr Hatton popped his head round the door of her office to smile and say good morning.

Voices came from the corridor and she turned to see Russell Nicaise standing in the doorway, a scowl on his handsome face. She stared in amazement at the fierce expression and the dark brooding eyes.

'And what good do you think you can possibly be today if you stay up half the night before a case like this?' he said.

'What do you mean? We had an emergency.'

'It's too much . . . you can't work all night and all day.'

'I'm all right,' she said, and smiled, her heart beating faster. He cared that she might be tired and overworked . . . he was being the gallant Frenchman, hating the fact that the petite woman should be made to work too hard.

'I can't have staff dropping half dead in my theatre while I'm concentrating on a new procedure. It isn't fair on me. I'm not all that sure what Sir Alec does and you will have to be told of every blessed thing we need, having never seen this operation. I wish that for once, a private hospital could accept the fact that they can't really cope with a full surgical load, and borrow staff from the relevant units.'

She felt her colour rise. The selfish, overbearing monster! 'If you must know . . .' she began, but he had walked furiously away before she could tell him that she knew what to do during the case. She set her lips and the hazel eyes were green for danger. 'I'll show . . . that self-opinionated creep what we can do.'

'And who might that be, I wonder?' The exaggerated Irish accent was full of teasing laughter. 'Not me, Nurse Clare.'

'Sir Alec . . . how good to see you.' She blushed. 'That wasn't for your ears. I've been looking forward to seeing you again. I think we're all ready. Have you any new ideas or anything I ought to pop in to boil in case you have to revert to another method? I've put in three sizes of sockets and joints if you have to do a modified Joudet, and the set I've laid up is the one you used when the Dutch and Americans came a few months back.'

'That's wonderful. I came here because I heard that you were the new sister. Don't think I'd trust this to anyone who doesn't know my terrible little habits.'

She smiled. 'I haven't been here long enough to make this a Beatties theatre, but I'm working hard on it. Some things are less than perfect, but I know you well enough to tell you if there is something happening beyond my control, Sir.'

She tied on her mask and saw the shattered surprise on the face of the man who had insulted her . . . and wounded her heart with his caustic tongue. It was easy to hate him now and to forget the warmth of his hand over hers, the passion bruising her lips in that stolen kiss. She joined the two men at the scrubbing bay and Sir Alec asked one or two relevant questions about the man coming into their care. 'We must show Mr Brewster that we can give him a hip joint that gives him mobility, no pain and no creaks,' he said. 'Ready, everyone? Let's begin.'

The patient was in a good position on the table, the high tray above the feet was laid with the instruments the surgeon would need and another was out of his way over the shrouded chest, leaving room for the anaesthetist to work freely. Russell Nicaise took up the scalpel and made the first incision, firmly and with confidence. As he needed swabs or forceps, they were ready to his hand; there were clamps waiting and retractors of the right size even before he knew he needed them and the flow of empathy that builds between surgeon and staff was smooth and warm. Even Nurse Adams moved fairly quickly and brought the right things at the right time, cooling boiled instruments in sterile water so that they didn't burn the hand they were put into from the trolley.

One hour passed, and then two, and they made good progress. Dr Hatton nodded when asked if 'everything was all right up his end' and Russell Nicaise concentrated on the absorbing task of achieving perfection. He had no time to think of the small figure by his side who anticipated his every need. He knew only that he could cut and make good, using the things handed to him, without having to ask for anything.

At length, Sir Alec looked up. 'Is anyone making coffee? I have to be back in Town as soon as possible, so I'll leave you to close, Russell.' He stepped back from the patient as he saw Nurse Price taking the coffee into the surgeons' room. 'There's service for you. Thank you, Sister. It's surely great to work with you again. Be careful, or that man there will be stealing you to take to Canada to scrub for his case there.'

'I'm very grateful to you, sir,' said Russell Nicaise as he held out a hand for the skin sutures. 'I know that I can do this with confidence both out in the Mendips and in Canada. Have you any pointers for after care?'

'Should be quite straightforward. Give me a ring tonight just to check. Goodbye, Sister . . . any time you want to do nothing but bones, let me know. I have a new theatre being built and I shall need a Beatties girl.'

Rosemary continued to hand the required material for closing the long incision. The surgeon seemed more aware of his surroundings, as if emerging from a tunnel. 'Thank you,' he said, gruffly. She made no reply.

Sir Alec came to the door, dressed in his immaculate suit once more. 'By the way, Russell, how is Caroline? Is she likely to come to England soon? You must be very pleased to be able to mix business with pleasure in Canada.'

'I shall see her here first. I had a cable saying she will be in Bristol in two days time. I'm sorry you'll miss her. I know she enjoyed meeting you.'

'Well, bless you both . . . bless you all, and thank you,' he said.

'I'll have the cases packed as soon as I can and sent to your car, sir,' said Rosemary, and Nurse Adams took the last of his instruments to clean and boil and dry quickly as the sister had instructed her. 'Good,' said Rosemary. 'You've been a tower of strength, Nurse Adams.' She smiled and the older nurse blushed at the unexpected compliment.

The patient was carefully lifted on to the trolley and transferred to the ward, Dr Hatton and Mr Nicaise going with him and leaving a trail of dirty gowns and masks behind them. Rosemary turned her stiff neck from side to side to free it of tension and gratefully accepted the cup of excellent, steaming coffee that Nurse Adams thrust into her hand. 'You're very good, Sister,' she said, and Rosemary knew how much it cost her to admit it.

'We were a real team,' she said. 'I couldn't have done it without the support of you two. You knew what to do and I had no worries about either of you.' They both looked so pleased that Rosemary thought that she could be excused a white lie! She had to talk, to work and to take her mind away from the man who had taken all her work for granted and said hardly a word to her since being rude. Mr Nicaise was going to see the woman from Canada . . . in Bristol, in two days time. I know that Sir Alec often says bless you all, but he had almost said it to Russell Nicaise as if he was blessing a couple about to be married.

Sir Alec had used the French pronunciation of Caroline which convinced her that she was French-Canadian and the fiancée or lover of Russell Nicaise. Rosemary finished clearing the instruments, checked what drugs the anaesthetist had used and made notes of everything done while it was all fresh in her mind. Dr

Hatton came back to mention a case being done during the week and drank two more cups of coffee.

'I need it if I'm to see patients in the Royal,' he said. 'You look remarkably well, Sister, considering what you have done during the past twelve hours.' He looked anxious. 'Don't make any decision about leaving us for a time, I beg you. I heard that Sir Alec was sounding you out to see if you'd be available for his new unit, but I hope you stay with us. I shall make sure that all the other interested surgeons know that you must have their full co-operation.'

'Please don't make a fuss, Dr Hatton. I shall stay for another month or so and then decide. The new unit isn't to be opened until the new year and that gives me plenty of time to make up my mind.'

It could be a life-saver. It only needed a word to Sir Alec and she could be back in London among her old friends and colleagues, working with men who appreciated her. Tears pricked her eyelids and she dashed the back of her hand across her eyes, furiously. I refuse to let that . . . that man upset me, she vowed. He left here without more than a feeble and very gruff, thank you . . . less than he said to either of the nurses. I suppose he thinks I was laughing at him when I pretended that I didn't know about the hip procedure or Sir Alec's work. A hint of amusement touched her lips. I suppose I was laughing . . . and it serves him right.

She sent Nurse Adams off duty for lunch and the afternoon. 'You can have a half day tomorrow, Nurse. As the theatre was cleaned thoroughly in the night and this was a clean case, we needn't wash walls again tomorrow and the sterilisers were turned out last night, so the bowls can be left ready to boil when needed. I've packed an emergency set in one of the large drums, so if an appendix or something simple came in, you could lay up and know it was all there for immediate use.'

'You mean I can do that even if you are off duty? I used to wait for Miss Nutford or one of the sisters from the wards to set out the instruments.' She smiled. 'The surgeons used to get mad because they didn't know what the different men liked and just guessed what was needed.'

'The mind boggles,' said Rosemary, dryly. 'In future, the emergency set will be sterile, with a list of the contents on the outside of the drum so that we can ask what extras are needed and add as required. Whoever puts them in to boil must be responsible for the cleanliness of the sucker tubings, in case one gets by without being flushed through after a case.' It was the first time she had referred to the blocked tubing she had found before preparing for the inflamed appendix and Nurse Adams flushed. 'I was very pleased with the way you helped me today, Nurse Adams,' she added, in a friendly tone. 'If you can stay here and work with me, I shall be very pleased.'

Adams looked at her in surprise. 'I enjoyed this morning, Sister . . . much more interesting than the usual run of cases we have here.'

The new sister folded a towel neatly. 'And if there were more cases like it and we had to use and care for a lot more complicated equipment, you would stay?' They stared at each other and in that long moment, Rosemary knew that the allegiance that Nurse Adams had for the Matron was fading fast. Nurse Adams nodded, and went back to her work, finishing carefully before reporting off duty.

'You already have a half day off today, Nurse Price,' Rosemary said. 'Take a long morning off tomorrow and come on at two. You've worked hard and I know you want to see your boy-friend. There shouldn't be anything for tomorrow, and if there is, Matron will have to send some help.'

'What about you, Sister? You look tired.'

'I am, but if I go off before Nurse Adams comes back, I shall fall asleep and be fit for nothing if we do get a case. I'll go off tonight and sleep the clock round.'

It sounded easy to organise the others and know that they wanted to go off duty, but what was there to do away from the theatre? It was Sunday in a fairly strange city, and she had no friend she could ring up and ask to go out with her. She tidied the drug cupboard and put two split airways out for sending down with a requisition slip so that the supplier would know the right sizes.

She went down to lunch and found Sylvia Nutford in the dining room. 'Come in and eat . . . you look a little pale round the edges. We seem to have a really good lunch today. Better make the most of it.'

'Is the food here always as bad as it seemed on my first day? I haven't had many meals here yet but it did seem very uninteresting.'

'Miss Dundry argues that most of the

staff are non-resident and shouldn't be encouraged to eat here. I've told her on numerous occasions that the food is bad, and that as there are at least eight full-time resident senior staff here, we should have better food.'

'Well, this must be what the patients are having today. It's delicious,' said Rosemary. 'I didn't know I was hungry until I smelled this wonderful sauce and saw the roast beef.' She helped herself to more vegetables. Sister Ridge was already eating and Rhona Brown, the radiographer joined them. 'Not working today, surely?' said Rosemary.

'Just a portable. Sir Alec wanted pictures of the hip to be sent back to him in London for his records.' She laughed. 'He could charm the birds out of the trees. I never work on Sunday if I can avoid it, but I was here last night and met him and he just couldn't be refused.'

'That sounds like Sir Alec,' said Rosemary and smiled. 'He's a lovely man.'

'I hear that Russell Nicaise did a grand job.'

'Yes . . . he was good,' said Rosemary.

'But he's not . . . a lovely man?' Rhona looked at her with mild enquiry in her eyes. 'I thought he could well be one of our leading bone surgeons in a year or so. The pictures show perfect alignment and no pressure. The patient has hardly any post-operative pain and should be walking very soon.'

'I doubt if he will work here for very long. He's half French and has firm connections in French-Canada,' said Rosemary. 'There is a lady coming to see him all the way from Quebec tomorrow or the next day.'

'Must be keen, but who wouldn't be? He's a very good-looking man and extremely attractive.' Rhona laughed. 'I often wonder if theatre staff feel attracted to the men they work with. It's a very intimate scene, isn't it?'

'Some are more attractive than others,'

said Rosemary. 'If they are bloody-minded, it doesn't really matter if they look like a Greek god!'

'And our Mr Nicaise is bloody-minded? I'm surprised.' She went to the hideous sideboard to help herself to well-cooked cherry pie and fresh cream. 'Miss Dundry must have had a brain storm,' she said.

'You all keep mentioning the food. Isn't this a typical Sunday lunch?' Rosemary was greeted with derisive laughter. 'In that case, I'll have some more before it all disappears.'

After lunch, she went to the annexe to fetch a book and some medical journals that Nick had left for her to read. It would pass the time on duty if she finished making out the dispensary list and the other weekend jobs that had been postponed because of the Sunday case. The air was summer-warm and yet the first leaves were changing on the chestnut trees of the Gorge. It would be pleasant to sit by the

Brunel bridge and watch the boats below on the curving river. She walked back past the secretary's office, now deserted, and went in to see if there were any messages for her. It wasn't very likely but sometimes news of admissions gave a clue as to future surgical lists.

She smiled. Miss Dundry was playing safe. The Thursday list for Sir Tristram Maloney was all tonsillectomies and minor nose operations, filling the beds but taking very little time in the theatre. It was a list that any third-year student nurse could take, given the right instruction. The hospital was nearly full and apart from two admissions for Mr Moody later, there would be no free beds for a while. She turned as she heard a step outside the door.

'Ah, Sister.' Miss Dundry smiled, sweetly. 'As you can see, we are getting very full. I know you have just had a day off.' She said it as if it was a week's holiday. 'But as we shall have no room for emergencies this week, I'd like you to take your next day off on Wednesday. That will leave you free for whatever comes in later in the week.'

'That's a very good idea, Matron,' said Rosemary. 'I was thinking the same way.' She looked at the older woman. 'Does that fit in with Miss Nutford? Or had you other plans about relieving me? I ought to make it clear now, Matron.' Miss Dundry winced at being addressed in any way that made her seem a working Matron and not a hostess. 'I should make it clear that in future I shall be sleeping away from the hospital before and after my day off, so that I can have a complete break.'

'Where will you go? I thought you were alone in Bristol.'

'I can visit friends and I might sometimes go back to London to stay at my old training school. I can stay in the hostel there.'

'I see.' She was obviously annoyed, but there was little she could do about what appeared to be a normal and reasonable request. 'Dr Hatton was talking to me and said he was satisfied with . . . Nurse Price helping him.'

'He was very pleasant to work with, Miss Dundry. He seemed very interested in the future of the theatre.'

'Yes . . . he asked rather a lot of questions, I thought. He even asked about matters that were of no concern of his, like conditions for staff here.' She frowned. 'He is a senior man, but I hope he isn't going to be difficult. He said he is coming to the committee meeting on Wednesday . . . he's never attended one before.'

Rosemary gasped. So that's why the food was better and Miss Dundry was all false sweetness. It was beginning to sink in that she couldn't run the place without the full co-operation of her staff and she might possibly have to make concessions. She watched the beautifully coiffured head as Miss Dundry went back to her room. And that's why she wants me out of the way on Wednesday! thought Rosemary. She thinks I might talk to the surgeons about conditions here, as well as the lack of necessities.

She glanced in her slot for any messages, not expecting to see any. A memo on the familiar pink paper was crumpled beside another note. She put them in her dress pocket and took them to the theatre. Nurse Price was ready to leave and had left coffee percolating. Rosemary sat in the surgeons' room and sipped the reviving brew while she read her notes. The memo was from Nick, who had telephoned and found her busy in the theatre. 'Going to the bone hospital with Russell Nicaise to watch him in action Tuesday. See you P.M. in the carvery?'

She smiled. It was wonderful. Never in a thousand years could Nick and she have anything more between them but firm warm friendship, but she was delighted to have his visit to look forward to. It would be the bright spot in her week and she would stay in the annexe. Even if she stayed, there was no need for Miss Dundry to know. The knowledge that her theatre sister might be away would at least set the train of thought that it was necessary to have someone on call and not to take it for granted that the theatre sister worked day and night.

The other note was folded and sealed lightly with sticky tape. She opened it. 'I want to thank you for your help today. It was only when we'd finished that I fully realised how much you contributed. As Sir Alec said, really efficient work seems simple to the layman, and even surgeons take too much for granted.'

Her eyes misted and her heart beat faster. He thanked me . . . he knows I'm good. So . . . it might have been Sir Alec who told him about her and stood over him to make sure he thanked her, but the facts were there and he accepted that she was a first-rate theatre sister. Her pleasure was limited. I know I'm good . . . I wouldn't have this job at this early stage in my career if I wasn't . . . and it's good to know that Russell Nicaise sent this recognition, but what of me as a woman? He will meet his beloved and forget the existence of the tiny woman who is nothing to him beyond another pair of intelligent hands.

She read on and her face hardened. So that's why he said nice things about her. She could hardly believe her eyes.

'I am doing a similar operation on Tuesday and your friend Nick is assisting me. Could you get a day off from the Birchwood and come and scrub for me? I could pick you up before the case and make sure you got back safely. Please ring this number.'

He would pick her up . . . to take her to work and put her down again as if dropping a discarded piece of paper into a waste bin. He knew she worked hard, but he had no hesitation in expecting her to give up all her free time and work for him, for grudging praise!

And isn't that what I would like? To be with him in every way . . . working, playing, eating . . . sleeping? I would work for him until I dropped with fatigue, if he loved me and not that girl from Canada.

CHAPTER SEVEN

'COME in if you want something, Nurse.' Sister Rosemary Clare raised her voice slightly above the sound of a highpowered lawn-mower that shattered the peace and made her wonder if the open window was a bad idea after all. She went to shut the window and turned to see who had come into her office.

'Don't shut the window on my account,' said Russell Nicaise. She turned away and fumbled with the catch, hoping that the rush of colour to her face and the rapid rise and fall of her bosom wouldn't give away the fact that his presence confused her. 'I tried to see you yesterday but you were at lunch and when I came back during the evening, you were off duty.'

'Even theatre sisters have to sleep

sometimes, or as you rightly said, they would be fit for nothing and . . . what was it? oh, yes, staff dropping half-dead in the theatre and not knowing what was expected for the hard-working surgeon.' Her blush could now be taken as a flush of anger and the brightness of her tear-filled eyes for dislike.

'You didn't exactly put me in the picture. Why didn't you tell me that you and Sir Alec were as thick as thieves?'

'I don't like that expression. I admire his work and am very fond of him as a person. He is kind and considerate and after the way I've been treated here, he was like a dear member of my family appearing in the doorway . . . a father figure.'

'Have you a father?' he said.

'No, I don't remember him . . . but I miss him.' She couldn't think why she said it, and bit her lip. Sympathy was the last emotion she wanted to encourage. Anything but sympathy . . . or pity. 'And you? . . . oh, I'm sorry. Your father was killed.'

'Yes, and there are some things one can never forget.'

Why did his words remind her of something? It was to do with the flowers he had sent. He must be a man to whom memories of a family nature meant a lot. He would never forget an anniversary, she thought with envy.

'You wanted to see me?' She was formal again.

'First to thank you and then to ask if you received my note. You didn't telephone me.'

'I'm sorry. I went off duty and slept from five o'clock until the next morning. Then I came back on duty and I've been so busy that I haven't had a chance to telephone.' She shifted some papers on her desk, but the empty theatre told of a slack time between lists, she was wearing one of the well-cut white dresses and white shoes and her hair had not been under a theatre cap since the day before.

'Can you come?' His dark eyes were intense and demanding. 'I need someone there who knows this operation.'

She raised her eyebrows and the corners of her soft mouth twitched with bubbling mirth. 'But you disapprove of staff from private nursing homes and hospitals assisting at major surgery. You wanted to make it a rule that special units should send their staff when a case had to be done in such places.'

He ran a hand through his hair and shook his head, the generous curve of his lips becoming a straight hard line. 'This is surgery, damn it! For God's sake don't get coquettish with me! Save that for Nick . . . if he can stand it.' He was close to her and she had to lean back against the desk to look up at his face. 'Are you going to help me or not?'

'I haven't the time off. I was told to take Wednesday off as we shall be slack until Thursday.' She looked up, her eyes full of appeal. Don't hate me, she wanted to cry. Can't you see, if I don't joke about everything you say, I shall fling myself into your arms . . . and that would be fatal. Her inner humour flashed into her eyes as she had a vision of his angry and embarrassed face if she *did* fling herself at him.

He saw the softened expression and the trembling lips. 'You are the most aggravating, funny child,' he grated. He took her shoulders and shook her so that her head went back and forth like a doll's. He lifted her clear of the ground so that all dignity fell from her and she blushed scarlet. His mouth sought hers in an angry, wild kiss. He put her down. 'Now behave,' he said.

'Will you please get out of my office,' she said, slowly. 'Isn't it time you went to meet a plane . . . or someone? How can you forget that a person in love can never kiss another person like that?'

He was immediately correct again. He

gave a stiff half-bow that made him more French than English. 'I beg your pardon,' he said. 'It was unforgivable in the circumstances.'

Her heart ached for her own wounded feelings and for his sudden compunction, but she knew that if he kissed her again and held her in that hard embrace, she would cling to him and return kiss for kiss, becoming ever closer . . . ever more in love. She took a deep breath.

'I'll be fair,' she said. 'I can't come with you, but I have just made a list of everything Sir Alec likes and everything I prepared for you. You can take it with you if you want it and if it will help.'

He took the neatly-written list and account of the procedure and read it carefully. 'Did I use synthetic ligatures at that stage?' She nodded. 'I didn't know. I only know that as I needed something, you were there.' His face was on a level with hers as he sat on the chair by her side. She brushed a tendril of hair back under her cap and wondered when her heart would break. Would the girl from Canada give him what he needed?

'This is wonderful. I shall take it to the theatre sister tonight. I know she'll be as pleased to have it as I shall. It's . . . very generous of you, Rosemary.'

'Think nothing of it . . . I have a copy and I shall enter it in the book.'

'That's not what I meant.'

She avoided his gaze. 'Haven't you noticed? Nursing staff are very helpful to the rest of the clan. I would expect others to do the same for me if I needed help.'

'And you are off on Wednesday? I would like to take you out for dinner, if Nick has gone back and you are alone.'

'There's no need,' she said.

'I am aware of that.' His irritation was showing again. 'There doesn't have to be a need. I want to take you out because I am very grateful and you were such good company when we went out with Clive.'

He took her hand. 'Let's get back to that, Rosemary. Let's be friends if we are to work together sometimes.'

'Will you have time? I thought that your visitor was coming.'

'Caroline?' It was the French way of saying the name again. 'She will be here for a flying visit on her way to London. She is playing in a concert at the Festival Hall. I shall see her after the tour before she goes back home. I am meeting her in the morning on Wednesday, I have been summoned to a meeting here in the afternoon and I shall be bereft and alone all the evening, and so I think will you be when Nick goes back.' He smiled. 'We have a duty to console each other . . . with good food.'

It was impossible to refuse him. If he went back to Canada she would never see him again . . . what did it say in Omar Khayyam? 'Unborn tomorrow and dead yesterday, why fret about them if today be sweet?' 'I'll be ready at eight,' she said, and handed him the papers in a long envelope. 'Good luck tomorrow.'

He took the envelope and raised it with her fingers to his lips. 'Many thanks, *chérie*,' he said, and strode away.

He got what he wanted from me, she thought with an empty heart. If I couldn't go with him, he has the next best thing and it will only cost him the price of a dinner and a few hours of his time when he will be glad to fill in the time after saying farewell to his lover. She was content to be alone, to go through the motions of tidying and packing drums and packs, making notes for drugs and lotions, and oiling delicate instruments before putting them in the glass-fronted cupboards. The whole hospital was peaceful in the corridors and she could understand why Miss Dundry wanted to keep it as a medical establishment with none of the rush and drama of acute surgery.

It isn't my kind of life, she told herself, making plans for going to London to

find out details of the new bone unit at
Beatties. It would be thrilling work and
she would have to lecture to nurses
approaching their final exams, and train
theatre staff as she had once been trained.
It was tempting and she resolved to find
out all she could about it and to ask Nick if
he knew more than the rumours suggested. She frowned. It was also what she
had left, quite deliberately. It would be a
specialist theatre with no variety beyond
the various orthopaedic operations. She
came away to have more variety, to meet a
wider range of surgeons and make a fresh
life in a different city. She stared out at the
trees and saw that the leaves were twisting
as if rain was expected. I have a different
city that could become my favourite town,
she thought. I have variety in my work
and I'm meeting people who are getting
on my wave-length and beginning to
know my worth, so why can't I settle for
that?

A few drops of rain fell on the window

and the smell of new-mown grass faded as she shut it fast against the storm. I can go back . . . or I can stay, but wherever I am, I shall take my heavy heart with me. A distant rumble of thunder made her go back to the window and look at the sky. The bridge would be awash soon, gleaming silver above the silver river. This could be my city, she thought and went to answer the telephone.

It was a relief to be told that Sir Tristram wanted to do a minor operation in the anaesthetic room of the theatre. Miss Dundry was almost apologetic. 'We had to find room for her . . . a daughter of a local member of parliament.' She paused for the right reaction.

'How old is she?' said Rosemary. 'Is she having a local?' She smiled as she pictured Miss Dundry who would admit any patient with a title or a very high position in society or politics even if it meant using her own guest room.

'Her grandfather was a Bishop,' said

Miss Dundry, sure of her proper priorities.

'Really?' said Rosemary sweetly. 'But you haven't told me how old she is, Miss Dundry.'

'She's five years old and her mother would like to stay with her.'

'Her mother can wait in my office if she likes, but there isn't room in the anaesthetic room for more than the staff involved. It would be very difficult,' she said. 'When is she coming up?'

'Sir Tristram is coming now. He'll send up his case and come back for Mirabelle. He likes to go with his little patients.' Rosemary had a feeling that Miss Dundry was not alone and she was exuding sweetness for the benefit of the anxious mother.

'We have a set of myringotomes here, Miss Dundry. I'll sterilise them with an auroscope. Do you know if this is a simple otitis media or will Sir Tristram need a pharyngo-tympanic tube? We have none in stock.'

'Oh . . . you'd better talk to him, Sister.'

'Sister? You have some knives I believe. I shall want very little. Just a simple case of relieving the pressure in the middle ear.' He listened while she repeated the questions she had asked the matron. 'No, never use them here. If we need that sort of treatment I take it to the hospital, but if you know about ENT I could do much more here.' Was there a note of speculation in his voice? 'You have some spirit drops? I prefer them to any other. I am convinced that they dry up the discharge more quickly than many of the other drops. And a little local will be all we need. They don't want to be here for very long. If you're ready, we'll be on our way up.'

Rosemary laid a simple tray with everything he needed and didn't wear a gown or mask when the child arrived, looking pale and tearful. She took the little girl and sat her on the table, giving her some bright paper wrappings that crackled as they were squeezed. Sir Tristram looked inside the ear while Rosemary held the child, and gently sprayed a little local anaesthetic into the opening. 'Good,' he said, and went to wash his hands. The tray was behind the child and she leaned back on the tilted head of the table watching Rosemary make a paper dart of the bright, stiff, shiny paper. Rosemary held her gently in the crook of her arm as Sir Tristram came up behind them with a tiny angled knife and the funnel-shaped piece of metal for putting inside the ear so that it exposed the tympanic membrane or drum. The light from his headlamp shone on to the inflamed membrane, and Mirabelle pulled away slightly, but relaxed when Rosemary murmured to her that it would make her feel better. The tiny knife made a short incision in the swollen membrane and a watery discharge flowed freely from the middle ear.

'Good girl,' said Rosemary. She saw

that Sir Tristram held the drops ready for insertion and she bent her head again to make a paper ship. Mirabelle was laughing when her mother appeared in the doorway and said she couldn't stay outside any longer. 'Come in,' said Rosemary. 'Look what we've made.'

'It's kind of you to play with her first to take her mind off it, but I'll stay while you do . . . what has to be done,' her mother said, dramatically.

'All over,' said Sir Tristram. He put a tiny wadge of sterile cotton wool just inside the outer ear to absorb the discharge and the superfluous drops. 'You can take her home now and bring her here to be cleaned up and dressed in the clinical room of the ground floor wing tomorrow.'

'But didn't it hurt?'

'What hurts, Mummy?' said Mirabelle. She clutched the paper models and eyed the rest of the wrapping material greedily.

'Would you like to take some home, and make some more?'

'Yes please . . . I can make some for my little brother,' she said.

Rosemary laughed. 'Isn't it funny how children would rather play with wrapping paper than the most expensive toys . . . cardboard boxes are a great success, too.'

The incident gave a lift to her mood and the rest of the day passed quickly, the storm left the trees glistening clean and the smell of wet grass went with her as she left the theatre for the night.

Sir Tristram was in the hall when she left and Miss Dundry quickly ushered him into her sitting room with his wife. The matron was wearing a smart suit of peacock blue that set off her white hair to perfection. It's a lovely life . . . but I have a feeling that it might change in the near future, Rosemary thought. It was possible to feel a tinge of sympathy for the woman who had ruled the hospital for so long and had enjoyed every luxury and advantage while doing so, but progress and the safety of the patients was what mattered most. The door closed behind the little group and Rosemary went to the annexe, to finish the unpacking that seemed fated to stay as it was for days if she didn't make a supreme effort. And tonight, it doesn't matter what happens, I'm going to wash my hair.

She hung up skirts and trousers and made a pile of creased shirts and summer dresses. The utility room downstairs was adequate and she spent a pleasant two hours restoring her clothes to the state in which she liked to find them. It doesn't matter what I wear off duty here, as there is nobody I have to impress, but she convinced herself that if she was meeting Nick, it would be unfair to go out with him looking badly dressed when he was taking the trouble to give her a meal and cheer her up.

With damp hair and wearing a comfortable velour leisure gown that reached the floor and made her look like a dressed doll, she sat by her window with a reading lamp shining warmly on the table before her. There was a bundle of glossy magazines waiting to be flipped over and she settled down with coffee and cakes at her elbow ready to relax for an hour before going to bed.

Photographs of willowy blondes with long legs and no visible hips stared out at her from the fashion pages, wearing clothes that would make anyone under five feet ten look like a Michelin tyre advertisement. She found some autumn clothes on one page . . . soft colours in good fabrics and just her style, with many garments that could be mixed and would tone in with the other garments in the range. They showed a long woollen dress of deep jade green with subdued gilt embroidery. This was modelled on a black jazz singer and looked superb. The next was a pop star, irridescent in shocking pink and black with the latest style in boots. Rosemary smiled. I'd look terrible in that, she thought.

She turned the page and saw a slim dark girl with long black hair and good skin. Something about her was arresting and made her read the caption beneath the photograph. She was wearing a scarlet kaftan and her delicate hands were covered with ornate rings. The hands were smooth and white as if they had never been in contact with anything as menial as washing up or other household chores. They drew the eye back again and again demanding attention. Rosemary read that she was Caroline Étave, concert pianist, who was commencing a successful tour with a famous orchestra with a first European appearance at the Festival Hall, England, her first visit from her home in Quebec. It must be her—the Caroline that Russell Nicaise is going to meet—the woman to whom he sent flowers to mark an anniversary. She saw the delicacy of her face and throat, the beauty of her dark eyes and the imperious set to the regal head.

He would never call her an aggravating, funny child, she thought, and a tear ran down on to one of the glossily displayed hands in the picture. If anything could convince her that Russell Nicaise could never take her seriously or to look on her as a grown woman capable of love and passion, this proved it to her beyond anything.

She cut out the photograph to save it, although she knew that each time she saw it, a knife would twist in her heart. I shall see him and be near to him on Wednesday . . . after she has gone, and then I may never see him again except in a professional situation. If he is to work in the West Country, I shall write to Sir Alec and accept his offer for the new unit. She went to bed, half dreading the day after to-morrow.

CHAPTER EIGHT

'IT had its moments,' said Nick.

'You didn't say much about it last night, but I suppose when Rhona Brown turned up in the carvery with her husband and insisted on joining us, you couldn't say a great deal,' said Rosemary.

'She does go on a bit, doesn't she? But I liked her. She could be a valuable friend for you here, Ros. You must meet people and create contacts if you are to enjoy a new city.'

'I doubt if I shall be staying for more than six months. I've been thinking, Nick. I do miss all my old friends and Sir Alec was very flattering about my work and offered me the new bone unit at Beatties. I'm going up next week to ask a few details.'

'I thought it was only on the drawing-board stage as yet. You can't say you'll take a job where the bricks and mortar haven't been laid.'

'It's further on than that. Sir Alec said it might be ready just after Christmas and he'd want me to move in sooner to order apparatus and stock, ready for the opening.'

'So you could be there before Christmas . . . say the middle of November or just later?' She nodded. 'That won't be very popular, Ros.'

'Oh, I don't know.' She shrugged. 'Seeing Sir Alec showed me quite clearly the contrast between the way Beatties surgeons act in the theatre and some of the men here. They expect very little from the theatre sister but act as if I'm not capable of supplying what little they do need.'

Nick reached up and picked a leaf from an overhanging tree. 'Not any more, they don't.'

'Nicely put . . . but untrue.'

'I was having a very revealing chat about you yesterday.' Her heart beat faster. 'Quite the mighty little atom, aren't you?' he teased.

She ran after him as he strode up to the observatory on the hill by Clifton Suspension Bridge. 'What did happen yesterday, Nick? Wait for me,' she panted.

They rested at the top of the path and looked over at the subtle leaf change that had crept up during the last few days. 'The operation was a success, eventually,' he said.

'What happened? Nick, you are being a bore!'

He grinned. 'Your name was on very illustrious lips more than once, suggesting that before he operated in that theatre again, someone in charge should watch you take a case similar to the one he was doing.'

'Not Russell Nicaise? No, Nick, I don't believe you. He still thinks I'm a freak.' The delightful blush that mounted on her

cheeks gave away her delight and surprise. 'Every time he sees me he treats me
as if I was a six-stone weakling with no
brain.'

'That's not the impression I had, and if
you value your life, you'll not put it at risk
by visiting anyone from that hospital.
They are sick of you without ever seeing
you.'

'I suppose you stirred it up, Nick.
That's nearer the truth.'

'It's possible,' he said, complacently,
'but we both did our share and got some
very dirty looks.'

'You are pigs. I know just what they
must have felt like. That hospital has an
international reputation and they can't be
faulted on their care and expertise. They
have imagination and compassion. I know
more about them than you know.'

'As from yesterday, you have an international reputation, too,' he said, with
a sidelong glance. 'We didn't know it
was happening, but a party of visiting

surgeons who were attending an international conference in London decided to come down for the day . . . Sir Alec told them about the case and they were too late to see the one he did here so he suggested that they watch Russell.'

'He must have had great confidence in him,' said Rosemary.

'He showed them your notes, and told them where you trained and where you now worked.' He grinned at her incredulous face. 'Can I be your agent when the little gentlemen from Japan come and beg the honour of you going to Tokyo to work for honourable chief surgeon?'

'I don't believe a word of it.' She looked up at the sky. 'The sun is just right. I shall now show you something beyond your comprehension! There's just time before you get back to the hotel to collect your bag. Read the notice . . . Did you ever see anything like it?'

Nick laughed. 'It reminds me of fairground stalls. All right, we'll go up if you promise to look after me. Sue will kill you if you let me fall downstairs and ruin myself.'

There were six other people waiting to go up the narrow, turning stairway and they soon heard the clatter of footsteps as the last batch came down. The room at the top of the tower seemed even darker than on the last occasion, as the outside light was brighter in contrast. Rosemary re-called the last time she had been there and brushed aside the notion that she was showing Nick the place where she had stood with Russell Nicaise because she wanted to be there once more . . . to remember his nearness.

Nick took charge of the overhead handle, amid giggles from three teenage girls who glanced at him in a provocative way and jostled to be next to him.

'I shall tell Sue you're baby snatching,' she whispered. 'Can't take you any-where.'

She was aware of a sudden rigidity in

his arm holding the lever. The girls wanted him to take the picture round to their friends who were waiting on a seat by the path, but he held it still. 'What have you seen?' said Rosemary.

'Nothing,' he said and turned the camera so that each section of the Down could be seen in turn. The girls giggled even more when they spotted their friends and called 'cooee' as if they could be heard from outside the tower.

'Take it back, would you?' said a man by Nick's other side. 'My wife and dog are by the bridge. I thought I caught a glimpse but you moved on too quickly.'

Almost reluctantly, Nick turned back. 'About there?' he said.

'No, further back.' The man took the lever and the scene flashed by quickly until the tower of the bridge was in full view. Cars flashed by in the sunlight, paused beneath the tower while the drivers paid for the toll and the red arm of the barrier went up between each car as the ticket was taken. A woman with a small dog looked up to see if she could make out any figures inside the tower and waved, hopefully. 'That's my wife.' The man seemed quite excited. 'Marvellous, isn't it. Tiny, but plain enough to touch, aren't they. Look at my dog. He's about the size of a small kitten from here.'

But Rosemary was watching a man and a slender dark-haired girl who walked by the bridge and looked up at the sweeping girders. They were small, as the man said, but everything about them was very clear. The girl wore a flowing coat of soft woollen material in a dramatic shade of purple, over a soft pink dress with flowing ties at the waist and throat. Her hair hung down in thick swatches, caught by some kind of ornate combs and her hand clutched at the arm of the tall, dark, wonderful man at her side. She raised her face to look at him and her eyes were wet with freely flowing tears. Russell Nicaise enfolded her in a protective and tender embrace and she buried her face in his coat.

'Let's see my friend again,' one girl said, touchily. 'You've had it on that side long enough.'

'You do it,' said Nick. 'Did you see who it was?' he said.

'You tried to stop me from seeing them. Thank you, Nick.'

'I'm glad you agree. Suddenly it seemed as if we were spying and as Caroline was crying, I felt that we should look away.'

'I'll walk back with you, Nick, and go on down the main road to look at some materials. I don't want to meet them.'

'Just as well. You'll be seeing him tonight, but if something has upset Caroline, I doubt if she would want to meet anyone, even one of Russell's friends.'

She smiled at him, gratefully, wondering if he suspected that she was falling in love with a man who was so utterly absorbed with the beautiful French-

Canadian pianist. 'I need never let him know we saw them if you will keep quiet, too, Nick.'

'It's probably concert nerves. What with jet-lag and butterflies in her tummy, that poor girl has my sympathy. I'm glad she could see Russell first. It will calm her and make her welcome to England.'

'Perhaps I'll leave a message that I can't see him. He might have had second thoughts about our date.'

Nick looked surprised. 'Don't do that . . . he needs a bit of consolation . . . don't we all.'

Rosemary saw him disappear into the dark foyer of the hotel and promised to visit Sue very soon. She walked down the road to the shop selling new autumn fabrics and patterns and lingered in the safety of the back of the long shop until she was sure that Caroline had taken Russell to the station so that he could see her on the train to London. Only then did she venture into a hamburger bar for lunch and to re-live the moving picture show that had forced itself on her unwilling sight.

The number of cars in the staff and visitors car park seemed more than usual for a Wednesday afternoon. Visitors came and went as they wished, only being asked to leave a bedside if treatment or examination was needed, and so there was no one time in particular when a large number came together. The admissions would be in by now and Miss Dundry liked to arrange flowers in the imposing front hall and to chat to patients being sent home or to doctors making their rounds.

But the cars that waited were mostly the status symbols of success in the medical profession. The glistening black limousine with the uniformed chauffeur waiting behind the wheel belonged to Sir Tristram and the Aston Martin coupé to Russell Nicaise. There were several other prestigious vehicles belonging to other doctors and surgeons and Rosemary smiled as she tried to match cars to owners. Dr Hatton had a rather shabby estate car built for utility rather than good looks, and useful for conveying loads of small children and dogs when he could tear himself away from his work.

What made them gather at one time in the Birchwood? Wednesday . . . of course, that was the day of the committee meeting. Rosemary paused on her way to ask for any mail in her slot and half turned away, suddenly shy of meeting any of them. She saw that the flowers on the main table were fresh, so it meant that Miss Dundry was ready long before the afternoon meeting, making her customary preparations to impress the men with her good taste and cultivated poise.

The few letters and a small parcel were soon in her handbag and Rosemary was glad that she had dressed with care. If she did see one of the surgeons, it was good to know that she looked as smart off duty as she did in the theatre. The pure silk shirt with tiny roses in the grey background was unobtrusive but right with the softly draped jacket and skirt of fine tweed, subtle with colours of pussy willow and reeds. Her high-heeled shoes picked out the grey again and matched her handbag and carried scarf. Once more, she convinced herself that she had dressed with such care in case Miss Dundry or one of the doctors came out while she was fetching her mail, but her eyes wandered towards the closed door behind which she knew the committee was sitting.

She heard the door open and hurried from the entrance, the absurd desire to escape proving overwhelming. If she was seen standing there, watching the door, what might be thought? She wasn't waiting for news of any possible outcome of argument . . . waiting to know her fate if Miss Dundry decided that she was too young and brash and conceited for the post she had accepted at the Birchwood.

Rhona Brown was leaving her car and called to her. 'Have they finished?'

'Finished what?' said Rosemary with an air of innocence.

'I'm not on the committee, but they are all there by the look of the cars. I wouldn't be in her shoes if she decides to be obstinate,' she said, and slammed the door. 'Just going to see Mr Brewster . . . not that I need any more pictures, but I like to see the end result. Why don't you come?'

'No,' said Rosemary, hastily. 'I just wanted to collect my mail. I don't think it's permitted to visit in off duty hours . . . it might be here, but I have hang-ups from my training school.'

'I'll pop in to tell you how he's doing, if you'll make me a cup of tea?'

'Fine,' said Rosemary. 'I'm not going out until later and I bought some rather nice pastries today . . . sheer greed and I can't possibly eat them all.'

'Great . . . see you later,' said Rhona.

The incentive to make tea for a friend encouraged Rosemary to make it as attractive as possible and she wished that the furniture in her room looked less like cast-offs from a jumble sale. She sighed. If only the staff were given better conditions and the quality of work was raised and expected, this could be such a good place in which to work. Perhaps it was as well that she wasn't too comfortable. It made her decision to go back to London much simpler. She stood by her electric kettle and twisted the lid of the tea pot, pensively. Nothing was *that* simple. I hate running away from anything, she thought, but what can I do if I have to see Russell and know that he can never belong to me? The tears of a dark-haired girl had moved him to such tenderness that Rosemary almost choked at the memory. Rhona's step on the stairs was a relief.

'Tea is served, Madam,' she called.

'Good. I can do with it. I nearly took pity on about ten very hot and bothered men who look as if they need some home comforts, but there would have been no cakes for us, and I'm starving.' She reached for a chocolate eclair and spoke through the crumbs. 'Bit of a showdown, I hear.' She laughed. 'I've never seen Miss Dundry so subdued. I don't know what was said, but I gather that they insisted on having a different accountant to make sure that any money is spent on essentials rather than on frivolities. The question of staff meals was touched on and there are to be changes there, thank God. I sent a note about that one. I do like good food if I'm busy here for more than a few hours at a time . . . and as for the resident nurses, they have very poor food.'

'Was the theatre mentioned?'

'I think that Russell Nicaise left in a flaming temper and your name cropped up somewhere . . . I'll get the rest from Clive when I see him. He, by the way, let Miss Dundry say her bit about ordering new curtains for her sitting room and the visitors' waiting room . . . all new last year, incidentally, and then he asked how much this would cost. She named a figure and he said it was roughly the figure he had in mind for a new diathermy machine in the theatre.' She nearly had apoplexy! The whole meeting took that tone and it was even hinted that it was time Miss Dundry retired and made way for Sylvia Nutford.'

Rosemary poured more tea but found it impossible to force down the delicious pastry on her plate. 'I'm very glad to have the day off, today,' she said, fervently.

'I thought you'd feel like that. As I passed the door, someone rushed out and asked the secretary if you were on duty.' Rosemary paled. 'It's all right. I said you were off for the whole day and not due back until the morning.'

'Thanks, Rhona. I couldn't face Miss Dundry today, if there's been a row. I know she will blame me if the men want changes.'

'Not before time. You haven't come here with any malice. That comes over, loud and clear, but you have made quite a stir, even with people like Sir Tristram who has been in her pocket for years. As for Clive Moody, if he wasn't safely and very happily married, I'd say he was falling for you!'

'That's very funny!' Rosemary shook her head. 'If you could hear him on about his family, you'd know that he could never look at another woman.'

When two people are in love, surely they can't try to flirt with other people . . . to kiss them, even in fun. She had seen Russell Nicaise with the pretty girl, hugging her and perhaps whispering words of love. How could he take the liberty of kissing another girl, especially when he believed her to be the girl-friend of one of his colleagues? The generous mouth and the dark eyes that could see insincerity in any other person didn't tell a tale of habitual chasing after women.

'I must go; I've a case to see at the convent and then I'm leaving everything to my partner for a few days. I might take in the concert at the Festival Hall if I can make it.'

'Do you have tickets?'

'Russell Nicaise gave me two, but said to leave them at the box office if I can't use them.'

'Of course . . . he'll be going.' And I shall fill in a few hours between one lovers' meeting and the next. It was almost unbearable to imagine meeting him again and talking of trivia . . . the weather and the progress the patient was making. 'Let me know how it goes. I'd like to go with you, but I think I'm going to have my hands full here if Miss Dundry throws a fit.'

'You have nothing to fear. I think you'll find that you can order exactly what you need and there will be no argument.' Rhona looked longingly at the last of the pastries. 'No, I'd better not . . . I'll never get to London if I don't pack now.'

Rosemary cleared away the tea tray and clipped the ends from the flowers she had bought from the flower shop along the road. She arranged them in her own pretty vase and put them on her dressing table, but the room still struck her as bare and comfortless. Someone tapped on her door. 'Come in,' she said, thinking it must be Sister Ridge or one of the other resident sisters or nurses.

'I've come to measure up for new curtains, Sister.' Rosemary stared at the housekeeper. 'All the sisters are having new carpets and curtains and some nice bits of furniture which have been in the store for ages. I've said often enough that it was a crying shame they weren't used, but suddenly, Miss Dundry came down to the linen room and told me to get on with it. You'd think the place was being inspected or something,' she grumbled. 'Mind you . . . it will look very nice when it's done. I'll say this for her, Miss Dundry has very good taste.'

Rosemary laughed and hoped that the housekeeper would not know why. Miss

Dundry must have had a bad scare to let her staff have anything she could use for her own comfort or channel to her facade of elegance. 'I was thinking I'd have to make some curtains of my own,' said Rosemary. 'I couldn't live with the existing ones for much longer.'

'Leave it to me, Sister.' She glanced at the flowers, the few ornaments and the two pictures that the new sister had arranged to the best advantage.

'I can see that you'll make it look very nice with your own bits and pieces. It's nice to have a pretty room if you're staying for a long time.'

She measured and left and Rosemary stood by the window, gazing out at the sky. Am I staying? she mused. I must decide soon.

CHAPTER NINE

'I THOUGHT we'd have an aperitif here before we go on to eat, if that suits you?'

Rosemary smiled. Whatever had been said in the committee meeting had not given Russell Nicaise any cause to despise her. In fact, ever since he arrived early at the door of the annexe, bearing a lovely bunch of cut flowers and waiting patiently while she took them to plunge the long stalks into a bucket of water until she had time to arrange them, he had been warmly polite, the perfect escort. She glanced at the almost stern face and noticed that he had dressed with care in smart casual clothes. The dark blue velvet jacket over a simple biscuit coloured shirt gave out ripples of dark richness as they passed under the lamplight, and she was glad that she had taken the trouble to dress well, deciding on changing her daytime suit for a soft dress of light blue under a silky black coat that would if necessary, shake off a sudden shower. He had glanced down at her shoes as soon as he saw her and smiled.

'Such tiny feet . . . but I'm glad you wear silly shoes,' he said. The smile took away any hint of disparagement and she had laughed.

'I shall have to treat you with care and carry you over all the puddles,' he said.

Tonight I shall enjoy being teased if he does it so gently, she thought. I will take and savour each minute so that when he is in Canada with his beautiful Caroline, I can re-live this evening as a precious treasure that will glow in my heart and comfort me.

'I shall be fine unless you want to walk in the woods,' she said.

'Is that why you wear sandals that cling to your feet by such tiny, breakable straps? It does make the perfect excuse to stay with the bright lights and forbid your escort a walk by the river in the moonlight.' He saw her smile. 'I remember you in more practical moccasins that you wore when we were with Clive. Did you think you were safe in the lonely woods . . . with him as chaperon?' It was said in a light, teasing voice, but she heard an undertone of tension as if he resented the fact that she distrusted him.

'I'd look rather silly wearing these shoes with that particular jump suit,' she said. 'Women do try to team up their clothes . . . and these are my "being-taken-out-to-dinner-shoes", worn with my second-best dress.'

They laughed and entered the hotel by the bridge. From the bar the lights from the bridge lit the terrace and they strolled out under the stars. He sighed. 'I had no idea it was so beautiful,' he said.

'Did you see the *Great Britain*?' she asked.

'No, there wasn't time.'

'I couldn't get there, either. I intended seeing it but Nick rang again and we went out for a walk by the bridge. He has almost the same obsession with it as you have.'

'And did Nick tell you about the hip job?'

'He said it was a success,' she said, demurely, smiling to herself as she re-called Nick's less than charitable remarks about the delays and mix-up of instruments by a theatre staff who had not only never seen the procedure in question but had never worked with the surgeon! 'I hope all went well . . . but at least you had a theatre geared to your work.'

'I deserve that. If it's of any comfort to you, I was lost without you. It's so easy to accept the best as the normal, until one has to make do.'

'I hope you were fair to them,' she said, gently. 'It isn't pleasant to be put in a false position, as I know. The staff there are first class and I'm sure did everything necessary.'

'You're right, of course, but I was finding my way too, remember, and needed an expert to hand me everything I needed before I even knew that I needed it!'

'And that, my dear doctor, is the life story of every theatre sister. She is expected to know what the surgeon needs before he has even decided what he's going to do! I often think I should boil up a crystal ball as routine so that I can see what is coming.'

'The girl scrubbed yesterday had hands as big as Nurse Adams' but she couldn't hold my big retractor.' He took one of her hands in his and smoothed back the silky frill that hung from the cuff of her dress. 'Such tiny hands and yet you had a grip of steel. Weren't you tired?'

Her hand rested in his grasp and she felt again the tender frisson of sexuality flow down her fingers. Surely he must be aware of it, too? It was heaven to be like this, on the brink of something, but it seared her heart to know that this was just the gallantry of a Frenchman, and was nothing to him. But tonight, he is with me and I can think of him as mine, if I don't allow my foolish heart to rule my head, and tell him that I love him. He led her to the edge of the terrace and they sat at a small table with their Martinis. Her fingers slipped from his and were cold without his touch.

'It's a knack, like lifting patients,' she said, 'It doesn't take strength, only balance and leverage.'

'I hope you aren't a Judo black belt as well as that,' he teased. 'Even with those slender sandals.'

She watched his eyes drawn to look at the bridge again. The sadness lurked behind a smile and she knew that she had seen that sadness whenever he talked of the Brunel masterpiece. 'What is it about the bridge?' she asked, softly.

'You know that my father died when planning to build one like it in Canada?' She nodded. 'Another man died with him and left a widow. She didn't suffer financially as they were already wealthy and he was an enthusiast like my father, but she was broken for months and we tried to comfort her.' He looked beyond the lights with the far away expression of one used to long distances.

'Who . . . you said we?'

'Caroline and me. Caroline has been staying near her for the last month while rehearsing and she said that she was helped.' He gave a gallic shrug and was suddenly very French. 'She is fond of Caroline and music.' He sighed. 'And now, she thinks she might marry again, a good friend of Marc's. It is what she needs, a man to love her and give her everything of himself and his strength.'

As you give strength to Caroline, she remembered.

'I sent her some flowers on the

anniversary of his death . . . which was also the death of my father.'

'You sent flowers to her?'

'Of course. It is right and I never forget. It is like putting flowers on the grave of my father, but it is better to give to the living,' he said, with crisp practicality. 'I wrote also, in case she believed that the flowers this year were a reproach . . . pointing out that she was betraying his love. I shall dance at her wedding and in a way it is good to be convinced that life goes on and must be lived with love and fulfilment.'

'And Caroline will help you,' she said.

'She came here and was overcome by memories. She loved them too. She does not share my reverence for the work of Brunel, but as I tell her, I shall never build a bridge and shall never be in danger from anything like it.'

'This is why you spend time looking at this view. I wondered,' she said.

'I want to show you the iron ship. Will

you come with me one day, Rosemary?'
She shivered slightly. 'You are cold. How
thoughtless of me. We should be on our
way and it's getting cool out here.'

'Where are we going?'

'Back to the lakes. Do you mind?' He
smiled, wryly. 'One can never escape
completely. I promised to look in at the
farm and tell them the result of the tests.
Young Michael made me promise to see
him as soon as he left hospital.'

'He isn't home now? Surely he'll need
nursing for a while?'

'He has a very good private nurse and
wanted to go home. As he has a wound to
be packed but isn't confined to bed,
there's no reason for him being in an acute
bed that should be used for a patient
needing care.'

'It will be late. Isn't he in bed by now?'

'We shall not stay for more than a few
minutes, but a promise must be kept,
especially to a child.'

He helped her into the passenger seat of

the low slung sports car and she drew the skirt of the coat closer round her, making a dark cocoon to protect her from contact with the man at her side. He looked down at her and smiled, his eyes glinting with amusement that held a background of tenderness. She broke the silence, wondering if she could endure this tiny space with just two people confined together, with the night wind rushing by as they sped along blackberry-sweet country lanes.

'This is smaller than Clive's car, but I suppose he needs one to take all those children about,' she remarked.

'One buys cars according to need.' The lights of the city were far behind and the cats eyes on the road shone with beckoning intensity, urging them on and on, hypnotically. 'When I need a big car to take out my family . . . when they appear, I shall use this one for nights when I am free . . . when I can drive out with the woman I love and leave *les enfants terribles* to a baby sitter.'

'You plan to have a large family?' Her mouth was dry. They would be dark and volatile with beautiful eyes. 'Have you always had your life planned?'

'No, when I came to England again and went to Edinburgh I worked and worked and had little time for any social life. I wrote to friends in France and Canada and made many friends among the medical fraternity here, but I made no plans beyond my career.' He slowed the car. 'And you, Rosemary? You seem very self-possessed and professional on duty and I know that your work means much to you.'

'Then you know all about me,' she said, lightly.

'Not all. Was there nobody at Beatties who brought a blush to your cheeks or made your heart beat faster? A woman as lovely as you must have attracted many men.'

I must hold on to the thought that he is in love with Caroline, she said to herself.

If I didn't know of his involvement, I could easily believe that he is on the verge of making love to me.

'Everyone falls in love when they go away from home for the first time. It is all so new and exciting and the men seem ten feet tall and very sophisticated compared to the boys at home with whom one grew up,' she said.

'And you fell in love?' He laughed. 'I was beginning to believe that you were incapable of letting your heart have any say in your plans.'

She looked at him sharply. If he thought that she and Nick had a love affair, he was being stupid. If he thought Nick was her lover, she *must* be capable of being in love. 'And now you have achieved a very enviable position in your profession,' she said. 'Everything is going as you want it. When do you go back to Canada and start phase two of your life . . . You are going soon, aren't you?'

'I plan to make two trips. One in

November to operate, and show the new technique, and one next spring when I hope to have a holiday there before coming back here to work, permanently.'

She gasped. 'I thought you planned to go back to your people.'

'The farm's up this lane, I think. What did you say? I don't think I ever told you I planned to work in Canada permanently.' Going round to her side of the car, he made sure there were no puddles where her feet would touch the ground. 'Come on, they'll want to see you,' he said.

'They don't know me and they won't want a strange female coming late in the evening when all they wish is to hear good news about Michael.'

'Come on,' he said, sternly. 'You can't bully me here, Sister Clare. I'm not in your beloved theatre now.'

'If you're sure it's all right?'

They walked slowly across the forecourt where one or two cars were parked and the concrete had dried after the rain.

'I had a long chat with Nick yesterday,' he said, casually. 'Nice guy . . . and very good at his work. We hope to get together a lot in the future.'

'That's nice,' was all she could say, but her mind rang alarm bells. Nick was very good at his work . . . and very good at chatting! She wondered if the conversation had remained solely about medical matters and some instinct told her that they had talked of other matters.

He rang the bell and a dog barked in the background of the house. There was a pause before someone came to open the door. 'Nick is very fond of you, Rosemary.' His eyes were enigmatic as he looked at the solid door and the brass letter box.

'Yes, Nick's a dear,' she said.

'Do you know, I have never been called . . . a dear.' His face softened into a half smile and steps came rapidly down the hall. As the door opened and a large golden retriever bounded out to greet them, she thought she heard Russell say, 'And if you ever call me that, I'll wring that pretty little neck.'

'Oh, there you are . . . how very good of you to come,' said Michael's mother.

'I hope we aren't too late for visiting,' said Russell, smoothly. 'We couldn't manage it earlier and I'm afraid we can't stay as I have another call to make.'

'Nothing bad, I hope?'

'Oh, no . . . an appointment I have promised myself for a long time but have been unable to make.'

Rosemary was introduced and they went into a room on the ground floor where Michael lay in bed surrounded by books and puzzles. He grinned happily when Russell went to his side and showed his bandaged leg. A chart that the nurse had made up before leaving for the day showed a normal temperature, sound pulse rate and no respiratory troubles. 'When can I ride?' said Michael.

'You'll have to let the discharge subside

more, but it's draining well. I told you all about it, didn't I, and I know you'll do whatever Nurse asks so that you can get well very quickly.' Russell turned to Michael's mother. 'The abscess is draining well and he is responding to drugs, so I think you have nothing more to worry about now. Michael can go to Outpatients at the hospital when Nurse thinks he is due for a check and after that, he should be able to ride again.'

Michael pulled at the sleeve of the blue velvet jacket so that Russell had to bend to hear him whisper. The whisper was hoarse and loud so that Rosemary heard it clearly. 'Is she the one?' asked Michael.

'Yes.' Russell nodded, solemnly. 'What do you think?'

'Yes,' said Michael '. . . she's all right.'

'What are you two whispering about?' said Rosemary, blushing. It was all very well to have a private joke at her expense, but it was embarrassing to have two sets of solemn eyes surveying her.

'Doesn't she know yet?' said Michael.

'Not yet,' said Russell. 'We have to go now, Mike. I'll see you soon. Be good,' he added, briskly.

'Goodbye,' said Michael. 'You'll come again with Mr Nicaise, won't you. I want to show you my pony,' he said to Rosemary.

'I can't promise,' she said. 'I work very hard and I haven't time to come out into the country very often.' She smiled. 'But I may see you when you come into Bristol, Michael. I'd like that.'

'You do like Mr Nicaise, don't you?' he asked, a trifle anxiously.

Rosemary looked up at the expressionless face that seemed to be waiting for the same answer. 'Oh, yes,' she said, airily. 'He's a dear!'

She saw a flash of a reaction that could have been humour or anger in the dark eyes. 'I think it's time we went. I have a rather troublesome woman to deal with,' said Russell.

'Was it something I said?' she asked with mock innocence.

In another few minutes, they were once more in the car, speeding towards the restaurant where they had eaten with Clive. Rosemary was conscious of a new tension between them that couldn't be fought with light banter. It was a relief to sit in the crowded place and be surrounded by movement and conversation. As she lifted the silver spoon to her lips filled with sweet melon soaked with orange juice and liqueur, she knew he was laughing, softly.

'I saw you gather your coat round you as a kind of protection in the car. Why are you afraid, Rosemary?'

'I merely wanted to keep it away from the door. I've had clothes ruined when they hung over the car doorway and trailed in mud,' she said, primly.

'*Je crois*,' he said. 'No, don't stop eating. I promise not to spoil your appetite.'

She bent her shining head over the plate

and tried to appear at ease, but a trickle of juice threatened to fall on her chin, and as she dabbed it with a corner of the linen table napkin, a quick glance showed that he was concentrating on his food. The meal progressed and Rosemary tried to eat slowly to postpone the time when they should leave the restaurant. 'Coffee? Oh, yes, please,' she said, to make the meal last longer.

'We'll take it out there,' said Russell and led her firmly to an alcove with a view of the lake, through a partition of green house plants. They made small talk until the coffee arrived and Rosemary was surprised that she could still pour from the heavy silver pot without her hand trembling. 'As I said . . . a grip like steel for such a tiny hand,' he said. She slopped the milk. 'Steady . . . you were doing so well . . . such perfect control,' he mocked, gently.

'If you can do better, you'd better pour,' she said.

'I don't think I could.' He reached over to take her hand. 'Feel my hand . . . it's trembling.'

'Don't be silly, it's as firm as a rock,' she said, trying to draw away. Oh, fix your mind on the woman he loves and try to hate him for being a lecher! she begged the gods, as if any of them could hear and help her.

'One of us is trembling. If it isn't me, then it must be you.' He drew closer and she could smell the musky fragrance of aftershave and masculinity. 'But that is impossible. Sister Clare is in complete control at all times, isn't she? Nick was saying how good you are at your job and that Sir Alec wants you to go back to take over his new unit.'

'Yes . . . I miss my friends in London and the Birchwood isn't quite what I expected.'

'But you have transformed the theatre and the whole place has had a shot in the arm since you arrived, in one way or another. There are going to be great changes there.'

'Like new curtains for the sisters showing that the hospital cares for the staff? That's just a sop to the committee.'

'Miss Dundry has decided to retire.' Rosemary started. 'Yes, she came to that conclusion when Sir Tristram asked her if she could use the pretty cottage on the side of the hill. It belongs to the trust that owns the hospital and is a very desirable residence. She can retire with dignity and say that she has to take the cottage now, or lose it.'

'I'm glad you were all kind to her. In many ways she has made the place what it is and it would never have had its ambiance without her touches.'

'But you still want to leave?'

'I don't know. I'm like Miss Dundry in a way.'

'Heaven forbid!'

'No . . . you know what I mean. I have the choice of staying on and continuing to build up the theatre and the goodwill between staff and surgeons or I can take the job in London among my friends. That job will be taken by another girl if I refuse now . . . so I haven't time to waste making up my mind.'

'You say you miss your friends? You can't stand still. There are other friends, other places to learn to love, Rosemary. Who will you miss? I know that you would see more of Nick in London.' He gave her a sidelong glance.

'Yes,' she said, too quickly. 'Nick.'

'And Nick is . . . "a dear".' She smiled slightly. 'And Susan . . . is she a dear too?'

'Susan?' Her eyes shot wide open and she looked like a startled rabbit.

'Yes, Susan,' he said, gently. 'You remember . . . Nick's fiancée.'

'You knew about them?'

'Only yesterday. He told me about her and showed me an interminable array of photographs. He is quite boringly besotted with the girl. I hope she's worth it.'

'Oh, yes, Sue is a wonderful person.'

'So, I am at last getting through the cobwebs of your life. I know that you fell in love at a tender age and I assume fell out again?' She nodded. 'Good. And now, you are busily building up barriers so that no man can interfere with your career.'

'No. I haven't met anyone yet who would let me continue my career after marriage.'

'If you fell in love, would that be important?'

'It might not be at first, but I love my work and I know that if I married someone and gave it up completely, I'd be unhappy after a while, knowing that I had something to give and could no longer do so.'

'So it follows that you'll have to marry a doctor or a surgeon.'

'Or stay unmarried.' She poured more coffee. Why was he torturing her? Had she given away the fact that she loved him, in spite of her efforts to keep it to herself? 'And what does Caroline want of life?' She had to face the fact that he was to marry Caroline, and she had to show him that she knew that he was philandering.

'Do you really want to know?' he asked. The dark brows were low and forbidding as if she had strayed into forbidden territory. So, she thought, it was quite in order for him to probe into her private affairs and wring her heart until her soul cried for mercy . . . and his love, but he couldn't bear to talk about the girl he loved.

'I've never met her and I wondered how a concert pianist copes with friendships and . . . love.'

'Caroline is younger than me. She is beautiful and a very pleasant companion.' He paused, the dark glance sapping away the will of the girl at his side. 'I love her dearly but she has to make her own life in many different parts of the world.'

'She is very beautiful. I saw her photograph in one of the glossies.'

'She's very brave, too. When Jean-Paul died, she began to think that everyone she loved would die . . . after all, she had seen my father die and with him, his friend.'

'Jean-Paul?'

'You don't know? I thought it was in all the papers. Reporters followed her until she was at screaming point and nearly had a breakdown. I spent a lot of time with her and hopefully, she is better, but when she comes to the anniversary of the death of her father . . . followed closely by the anniversary of the death of her husband . . . she suffers . . .' he said, softly.

'Her *husband*?'

'They were married for only a year and he was killed in a road accident.'

Rosemary was torn between incredulity and pity. 'So you must comfort her.' It might explain why he still flirted with her . . . and probably with other women. If she depended on him and he was not content with the widow of another man, there would be tenderness . . . but gaps in the relationship.

'I comfort her as well as any brother can do, but she needs a man to love . . . as a lover.'

'But can you not give her enough to make her happy?'

'Have you any brothers or sisters?'

'What has that to do with it?'

'Caroline is my beloved sister . . . one of two sisters and two brothers, all of whom you will meet if you are good.'

'Your *real* sister?'

'What have I been trying to tell you?'

'But I believed . . . I thought that you and Caroline were lovers.'

'*Mon Dieu! Tu es folle, ma chérie.*'

'Well, how was I to know? I saw you with her near the bridge and she was weeping in your arms. I thought she was sad because you couldn't be together all the time and she had to go to London without you to the concert.'

Her two hands lay like imprisoned

birds in a strong brown cage of tenderness. 'Such a little girl, with such strength and fire . . . ready to fight the world and yet, so scared. Why are you still frightened of me, *mon amour*?' His head blocked out the light of a stained glass lantern half hidden in the foliage behind them and his lips sought the softness of her trembling mouth. He freed her hands and they stole like soft flowers over his shoulders and round to the back of his leonine head. Her body felt as if it must dissolve in an ecstasy that was half pain and half joy as his hands caressed her slim body.

The sound of footsteps on the tiled floor brought them back to sanity and they sat side by side, holding hands while an elderly couple sat at the next table and drank Irish coffee. It looked so banal and ordinary as if the earth hadn't moved off its axis for a tiny span of timeless enchantment. 'Do you know,' said Rosemary, with a smile that threatened to dazzle the stars, 'I think you're . . .'

He looked ferocious. 'Careful . . . or I'll disgrace you in front of these solid citizens.'

'I think you're a darling, darling man,' she whispered.

THE END

THESE ARE THE OTHER TITLES
TO LOOK OUT FOR
THIS MONTH

THE SLEEPING FIRE by Daphne Clair

Adam Broome – the 'new Broome' as he soon became to all the staff of *Lively Lady* magazine – was living up to his name and introducing all kinds of changes, and editor Lee Palmer wasn't sure she was happy about them. She felt happier about Adam himself, who was undeniably attractive. But then she wasn't the only one to feel that way about him, was she . . .?

RELUCTANT PARAGON
by Catherine George

Since she had been widowed six years ago, Eleanor had been very cautious about her relationships with men; they were only too ready to assume that all widows were merry ones! And James Ramsay was precisely the kind of man most likely to jump to this conclusion. So Eleanor decided it might be best to leave him with his wrong impressions about her. . .

EACH MONTH MILLS & BOON PUBLISH
THREE LARGE PRINT ROMANCES
FOR YOU TO LOOK OUT FOR,
AND ENJOY. THESE ARE THE TITLES
FOR NEXT MONTH

———————— * ————————

LESSON IN LOVE
by Claudia Jameson

MAKESHIFT MARRIAGE
by Marjorie Lewty

THE MAN SHE MARRIED
by Violet Winspear